Gemini Jones

"My Past Came Knocking" -The Savannah Wooten Case

VERONICA FAYE

ISBN: 1475142366
ISBN 13: 9781475142365

Chapter 1

The Day David Ban Went to be with His Ancestors

State Senator David Ban had just announced his candidacy for governor when the first bullet tore through his chest, making sauce out of his heart. The stunned man first looked as if he had seen a ghost. He turned to look at his wife, Glenda, when the second bullet hit him and made a mess of the left side of his face. The crowd that had come to support him realized what was happening and chaos broke out. People started screaming and running for their lives. The police reacted as quickly as they could but not before the shooter fired a third shot, hitting the already dead man in the left shoulder. David Ban was dead before he collapsed into his aides' arms, sending blood all over her Co Co Channel suit that she had bought just for this occasion.

Savannah Wooten did not try to resist when police approached and told her to stay where she was, as they removed the gun which was lying at her feet. She merely stood still as police surrounded her, grabbed her hands behind her back, and handcuffed her. She went quietly with them to the awaiting police car as fans of the beloved politician screamed at her, "Why did you do this!" Savannah never looked back or said a word.

The momentum of the crowd, the anger and the shock, grew and they shouted to Savannah, "Why," "Traitor," "Murderer," as they led Savannah away. A group of twenty or more policemen arrived on the scene to prevent yet another murder, the murder of the suspect.

Camera crews and reporters from the various TV stations and newspapers began to swarm around the police and Savannah, bombarding her with questions and ignoring the police demands to step back. Savannah held her head high through this ordeal and remained calm even as the crowd started to shout for her death and for justice. What seemed like hours to get her to the awaiting squad car only took a couple of minutes, but the five police who surrounded her finally got her to their mutual destination: safety.

Once inside the car, her only statements were that she was glad the son of a bitch was dead and that reading her her rights was not necessary; she would tell them what they wanted to hear.

Now it was bad enough that this happened in front of the community center that Ban had established five years earlier; it also happened in front of three TV station film crews, as well as every major newspaper reporter in the city.

David Ban was rushed to Community Hospital but it was just a formality, he was dead at the scene. His body was then taken to the county morgue where the medical examiner would determine which gunshot ended the beloved state senator's life. His wife and several of his aides were treated and released for shock. Savannah Wooten was taken to an area police station, fingerprinted, photographed, and placed into a cell. She had not uttered a word to police since being placed in the squad car, but had verbally confessed to wanting David Ban dead and to killing him. She then asked for her one phone call to talk to the lawyer who would represent her.

Officials, fearing that she would attempt suicide, placed her on suicide watch.

Gemini Jones

I was born on the coldest day in Gary, Indiana history, January 6th. Why my parents named me Gemini even though I was born under the sign of Capricorn, I'll never know; but my birth certificate reads Gemini Alexis Jones. It all seemed to work out later because at the are of twelve I was diagnosed with a mental disorder that would later be labeled bipolar disorder.

I come from a long line of people who were "crazy." One in every ten descendants of Cornel Jones of Pleasant Union, Tennessee was off centered. That means crazy, it just sounds better.

Although being bipolar can run in families, it is often triggered by a lot of stress or by some tragedy that the person goes through. In therapy, I learned that my illness occurred as a result of witnessing the death of one of my childhood friends at the hands of his father.

Willis Harvey was my best friend; he lived next door to us and we were always together. His mother, Rose, was one of the nicest parents on the block and she would always let Willis come and play in my yard, but he would always have to be home before his father, Carter Harvey, came home.

Mr. Harvey was not a very nice man and I used to overhear the grownups talk about him being abusive to Miss Rose and Willis, but I never knew what that meant until the day he killed Willis.

It was the Saturday before school was to let out for the summer. School ended on June 1st, which was also Willis' birthday. I had saved up some money from collecting bottles in the neighborhood and I had bought Willis a GI Joe because I knew that was his favorite toy.

As usual, Willis came over that Saturday to play while Miss Rose hung her wash on the clothesline in their back yard. Willis and I were fascinated with butterflies and other insects, so we took two jars, poked holes in the tops so the insects could breathe, and started trying to catch butterflies; we would study them and then let them go.

It was later told by the newspapers that Carter Harvey had been fired from his job for drinking and had come home earlier than expected. When he discovered that Willis was not at home, he came over to my house to get his son. My mother was in the kitchen preparing lunch for us when she heard the screaming from next door. As she came to the front door, she could see Mr. Harvey coming across their yard toward our yard and Miss Rose running behind him begging him to stop. My mother came out of the house to see what was going on but before she could say anything to them, Mr. Harvey was in our back yard yelling and cursing at Willis. I can still smell the alcohol on his breath even now because I still have nightmares about the event. Willis was a pretty good runner. In fact, he was the fastest kid on our block; but that day, his feet did not work. He froze as his father came near him and yelled at him for disobeying his orders about leaving the house.

I watched as he slapped Willis across the face, which sent him to the ground. He hit his head on the tree stump that my father was always saying he needed to get rid of. The blood splattered everywhere, and I remember the cracking sound as Willis hit his head. Then, Mr. Harvey did something I will never forget, he stomped Willis in the face, and I heard the cracking sound of his jaw and saw teeth fly out of his mouth. Miss Rose was scratching and biting and screaming at her husband while all of this was going on. My mother ran in the house and called the police, but some of the neighborhood men had come to the yard by this time and they were holding Mr. Harvey back.

I just stood there in shock, feeling so helpless that I could do nothing for my friend. Then I did something that even astounded the grownups. I ran over to Mr. Harvey and I kicked him between his legs and I screamed and screamed and was still screaming when my mother came back and grabbed me and took me inside. I later learned that Willis died before he could reach the hospital. Mr. Harvey was arrested and then released months later. He was not present at Willis' funeral, and shortly after his release, he moved out of town. Miss Rose moved in with her family and we never saw her again.

My parents and I attended Willis's funeral and when I went to see my friend's body, I placed the GI Joe that I had bought for his birthday inside the casket with him, and then I fainted. I was nine years old…

Then, at the age of twelve, I was diagnosed with the illness that would be a thorn in my side for a great deal of my life. But not an excuse…

I managed to make it through Carver Elementary School with only one fight under my belt. Trouble is I beat up everybody in my class, including two students who came in just to watch. I was always a little moody. I was really upbeat one minute, depressed the next. But it took beating up twenty-five of my classmates, including the boys, for the grownups to see that "Gemini was crazy as hell."

I was allowed home schooling for the rest of my 6th grade year and after medication and counseling, I was sent to Pulaski Junior High and then Horace Mann High School. There were times when I thought that I was able to go without taking my medication and that often got me into trouble. When a person is bipolar, mood swings are a common occurrence. After taking the medication for so long, a person can get a false sense that they no longer need to take their medication.

During my manic state, I was often up all hours of the night, partying with my friends, experiencing drinking and drugs. I fought a lot too. I could have given Mohammed Ali a run for his money when I was in my manic state. And I was unusually sexually active during that stage. I was always stealing money from my parents to go shopping. Once in my manic state, I was so bad that during a shopping trip with my mother, I jumped from the third floor of the mall to the first floor so that I could get to J. C. Penny's before it closed. I broke both of my legs and had to be hospitalized for weeks. The fights that I got into were so bad at school that after a while no one would mess with me. Several gangs tried to recruit me because they thought I was crazy. I was crazy, but only a few people knew it since I had no close friends. It was my school counselor, Mrs. Mattie Rufus that finally got me on the straight and narrow. She literally saved my life.

I remember the day she called me into her office. I was in the ninth grade and barely making it. She had my school folder that had followed me from grade school on her desk. She knew about my medication and after I admitted that I was not taking it, she talked with me about her sister's battle with depression. For the first time in my life, there was someone who I felt a connection with.

For the rest of the year I went to see Mrs. Rufus twice a week and it was on one occasion when she asked me if I was interested in going to a vocational school for broadcasting. She said I had a great speaking voice and when I said that I would try it, she set me up for an audition.

I remember the day she called me into her office to let me know that I had been accepted. I cried and she cried with me.

I did well in school after that. My medication and Mrs. Rufus were the reasons why. Life seemed to be clearer to me and I made plans for my sophomore year. I found time to get a job.

I was working at the local McDonald's that year—it's a very popular place where retired men come and eat every morning so the place was always crowded. I was working the morning shift, I like that shift because the customers were regulars and something was always happening during that shift. They were either auguring about current events, dating young "gurls" or they were gossiping about the troubles of the guys who were absent. Those old men were hilarious! After working my shift, I would go directly to school to take the bus to the Career Center, then in the afternoon return to Horace Mann.

Maurice Haynes saw me before I saw him. Maurice was one of my old sex partners from my days when I wasn't taking my medication. I almost didn't recognize him but then those days were a haze to me. He tried several times to get my number, but I explained to him that I had gotten myself together and wasn't interested. That did not stop him. He continued to bother me every day, trying to get me to go out with him. Finally, after a few weeks, he stopped coming into McDonald's and I thought my worries were over. They weren't. Maurice raped me two days later.

Years later, I attended Indiana State University majoring in Radio, TV, and Film, although I had no plans to pursue a career in this field. I just wanted to prove to myself that despite my "problem," I could go to college. I managed to maintain a 3.5 GPA there with the help of God, medication, and counseling. After my undergrad degree, I decided to get my master's in Public Administration. Hell, I was on a roll and Medicaid and I knew that I was destined for success.

Okay, you know what's next. Yep, I continued through school, having been accepted at Valparaiso University's School of Law. I did well there, although I did have a setback and spent the summer of my second year of law school in the hospital. I was not taking my medication and got into a fight with my ex-boyfriend, Jeffery, his new girlfriend and her mother, sister, and auntie with the cheap wig. No one pressed charges, and I spent time that summer preparing myself for that final year and getting rid of thoughts of killing Jeffery in his sleep.

My parents, Lena Mae and Cornel Jones, were my rock through all of my problems. My illness had somehow skipped my daddy, but it had manifested itself in all of his brothers and sisters to some degree. My uncle, Artis Jones, was in prison for killing a man that coughed without covering his mouth while Artis was eating catfish, spaghetti, and coleslaw, a Midwest Friday dinner favorite. Uncle Artis had the most severe case of "the problem." My other two aunts and two uncles were not as severe as Uncle Artis, but they had their ways also. My Auntie Della could never keep a man; they all seem to run screaming into the night, usually because she had beat the hell out of them. Her daughter, Natta, was usually very quiet, but once took an axe and busted out my Auntie Della's windshield of her new car, just because Auntie Della asked her to turn down the TV. She hadn't been taking her medication either. Auntie Della's other son, Darren, was okay; the illness skipped him. My Uncle Delbert was troubled but never got into any trouble. My Auntie Virgie killed herself my senior year in high school, she was in a depressed state after her husband left her for a woman he worked with. That was bad enough, but she killed herself at their wedding, shooting herself in front of everyone.

I was the only child, so my parents were spared the ordeal of dealing with multiple children with the same illness.

After law school I got a job at the public defender's office where I used my enthusiasm and knowledge to defend the underdogs in society, those who did not have the money or means to secure good legal counsel. I made a name for myself, mostly by getting my clients' charges reduced. But the case that caught the eye of the largest law firm in the city was a case of a black woman who suffered from the same illness I did.

Gayle Henderson was a 48-year-old sista who worked for a large accounting firm in the city. Gayle was responsible for processing the payrolls of several small companies in the city, a job that she was very good at doing. Gayle loved her job and had no problems with the stress of her duties, until the firm decided to hire Huang Cho. Cho was a Chinese immigrant with a working visa who spoke English with a heavy accent, who was hired to be Gayle's boss.

Gayle had also been diagnosed with bipolar disorder but was taking her medication regularly and doing well; until two years ago when Cho was hired and Gayle's medication needed to be changed. The doctor did not see the need to switch her medication, which would later be the basis for my defense.

Cho was good at what he did, that was not the problem which caused Gayle to bash his skull in one morning. The problem was that Cho was always sending her e-mails and not waiting for her to open them. He would usually write the e-mail and then yell to Gayle since his office was next to hers. "Guile, de you git my e-moil?" he would ask, not giving her time to access the message. This meant that she would have to stop what she was doing, open the e-mail, and answer him.

Now, Gayle is what you call "detail oriented" and very focused. So, to be interrupted like that several times a day was more than she could bear. Gayle had to meet several deadlines a week so time was precious and she had little time for interruptions. Most people knew that Gayle made time in the evening, an hour before she left for the day, to access her e-mails and respond to them. Most people respected that, Cho, however, did not understand the process, nor did he understand that aspect of Gayle's personality. This went on for two years, morning, noon, and, sometimes, just before she went home for the evening. She could not understand why he did not just come to her office and tell her what he wanted, but the reason was that Cho did not speak very good English and felt very uncomfortable talking to people. He found it easier to write down what he wanted to say. The trouble with that is that he wrote the way he spoke. For instance, instead of writing, "please advise," he would write, "please advice." This really irritated Gayle to no end, but as long as she was medicated, Cho was safe.

The day that Gayle bashed Cho's skull in and was charged with attempted murder was a very bad day for her. First, as I stated, Gayle and I suffered from the same illness, bipolar disorder, and the medication that Gayle was taking needed to be changed. Secondly, the bus that she usually took to work never came, forcing her to walk to work, which was two miles away. Thirdly, during her walk it began to rain and ruined the $75.00 hairdo she had just had done the past weekend. Everyone knows how sistas' are about their hair, so by the time she got to work, an hour late, she was ready to explode. Cho gave her the perfect opportunity to do just that. As she came into the office, the other members of her staff took one look at her and decided that she should be left alone for the rest of the morning—some thought for the rest of the year; or just before they announced their retirement, whichever was longer.

The crazed look in her eyes and the hair which was dripping wet and without one curl was the other. As she passed by Cho's office, she could hear him at the computer typing away. She had just removed her coat and was about to sit down when she heard the words that would change her life, and Cho's, drastically, "Guile, di you git my e-moil?"

Gayle's mind snapped. Witnesses said that it took less than a second for her to walk over to Cho's office and beat him within an inch of his life with the star-shaped paper weight/award that read "Good Job" he had on his desk. It took three men to pull her off of Cho, who was later rushed to the hospital where he remained in a coma for weeks. Security was called and then the police who took Gayle down to area booking and filed attempted murder charges on her. Before my arrival, she had been moved to the prison hospital to be assessed by the staff doctor.

Gayle's case was assigned to me, and it took less than a minute to realize that her doctor needed to be consulted to see if there was a chance that she needed her medication changed. If so, that would be my defense. She was extremely agitated and could not stop walking and talking. I asked her if she was bipolar, and knew from her reaction that she was. She was not making any sense, which was another indication that either she was not taking her medication or it was not working.

My boss wanted me to plea bargain down to assault, but I thought that I could win the case. After having Gayle's doctor examine her and consulting with his findings, it was decided that at the time of the incident, Gayle's medication was not working properly. I did convince the jury that Gayle's medicine no longer worked and that if her medication had been right, she would never have tried to kill Cho since she took her medication religiously. This case caught the eye of my future employer and reunited me with my past.

I got a job at Lyman, Webber & Strain, the largest firm in the city. I defended mostly drug dealers, which I didn't enjoy but I knew they deserved to have legal counsel under the law. Sometimes I had to defend car thieves, burglars, and other petty criminals, but it was my work with the "ray rays" of the city that got me the reputation of being a good defense lawyer. Word on the street was that if you sold drugs to the "po po" at twelve noon in front of city hall with two hundred witnesses present, Gemini Jones was the lawyer to get. I got a lot of my clients off or the charges reduced, depending on the circumstance and the ADA that I had to deal with. Most ADA's don't want the case to go to trial so I did a lot of plea-bargaining. But if I thought I could win based on the evidence, I usually went to trial. My record was a good one; in three years, I only lost three cases. But I was not the rising star of the firm and it looked as if my career at Lyman, Webber, and Strain was going to consist of defending "ray ray" and "June bug" forever.

It was while I was celebrating one of my "ray ray" victories at Walter's Bar and Grill—I was drinking mineral water with friends—that I saw the news story of Savannah Wooten and David Ban. I tried to remain calm while viewing the news, but I could not contain my surprise. I was visibly sick. Everyone in the bar was talking about it; a few people had been present when the shooting occurred and commented on how calm Savannah looked when the police surrounded her. She had been the guest of Ban's wife so she had not been searched by security. I could not stand to hear anymore, so I quickly got up, said my goodnights to everyone, and practically ran out the bar. I thought that I was going to faint, but managed to hail a cab to take me home. My dog, Kyrra, was eagerly awaiting me when I got home but I was in no shape to take her for her daily walk, I just sat on the couch in a daze. The demons from the past were coming to haunt me. Hell, they had a security deposit and first and last month's rent with them. They were coming to stay.

It came as no surprise to me when the next day I was called into Quinn Lyman's office and told that he had chosen me to defend Savannah Wooten on a first-degree murder charge. To think that the senior partner of the firm had chosen me wasn't a shock and definitely not a blessing. This was the kind of case that careers are made of.

Savannah Wooten was accused of killing David Ban, the most beloved African-American politician in the state. The motive for the killing remained a secret and was known only to Ms. Wooten, who, according to my boss, had not revealed to anyone.

"You know why; don't you, Gemini?" the demons in my head asked mockingly. You know why David Ban is lying dead on some undertaker's table right now."

She had allegedly shot senator Ban during the televised press conference...

"That's why I chose you to take this case," Mr. Lyman informed me this morning. "You are the best at getting clients off with the weight stacked against them. We're getting a large fee for this and I want her to have the best. You are going to have a fight on your hands; for one, she does not want to plea bargain. Secondly, she has not revealed to anyone why she killed the senator. And third, he was loved by everyone in the city and, reportedly, just about everyone in the city saw her do it. The DA is getting pressured from the mayor to make this trial short and sweet, but if I know Omar Robinson, he is going to make this case his stepping-stone for the governor's race next year so the ride is going to be long and hard. He will probably go for the death penalty."

"I take it that this is to be a priority one case. What about my other cases?" I asked, already knowing the answer to my question. I wanted to say, *"I can't take this case because everything I have worked for my whole life is at stake, so get somebody else; my ass is on the line here!"*

"We are reassigning all of your cases to Jason Wheeler. He is in the doghouse for the way he handled the Perkins case. It was sloppy work on his part, he was told to plead it out, but he let his ego get the best of him and now the client will spend fifteen years in prison."

The case that he was referring to was the Dana Perkins case. Dana Perkins, a 32-year-old mother of three, was accused of killing her children's father at the daycare center where Dana worked and the children attended. It was never established that Dana was a victim of domestic violence and suffered from battered woman syndrome. The ADA wanted to plea bargain the case from manslaughter one to manslaughter two, which carries a sentence of three to six years max. Jason, however, convinced the client that he could get her off, even though the ADA was willing to go lightly. Despite orders from the partners, Jason went to trial and lost; the jury found her guilty of first-degree manslaughter and sentenced her to fifteen years in prison. So as punishment for disobeying orders and losing the case, Jason Wheeler, the rising star of the firm, was banished to defend the "ray rays and June bugs" of the drug world, while I, Gemini Alexis Jones with the "problem," was just handed the case of all cases and the third biggest challenge of my life (the first being a black woman in America and the second being bipolar).

"Quinn, Savannah Wooten and I have history. Do you think I am the best choice?"

"I know that you and Ms. Wooten have worked on several charitable committees together," Quinn replied. "That's why we chose you; we figured she would feel better with someone that she knows and trusts. Don't worry, Gemini, the partners have faith that you will deliver. You will have the best legal team at your disposal. I am asking Antoinette to do your research and Bookie to do the legwork. Four paralegals will be at your disposal. You have the best. The decision has been made."

I agreed to take the case, but not for the reasons he thought. I had my own reasons for taking this case. I knew that this case was not going to be easy, that the lives of a lot of people were going to be affected, including my own. I would have to be on top of my game, which meant another trip to the doctor to review my medications and trips to my shrink, a sista named Dr. Elmonda Gray, to keep my stress level down and my head clear. This was going to be a test of my endurance, my sanity, and more importantly, it would bring back old demons, demons that I thought had long disappeared but were coming back with a vengeance.

I made it to the county jail where Savannah was being held. The press was everywhere, but no one stopped me since they did not know that I would be handling the case. I was greeted at the door by the detectives assigned to the case; two white men named James Harries and Harold Cartier, who both felt the need to tell me that I should plea-bargain this one out because it was a done deal. I paid no attention to them and asked to see my client.

Savannah looked as if she had just stepped out of an Ebony Fashion Fair show. Her Manny Couture suit was violet, a color that suited her flawless, paper bag skin color. Her hair was thick and shiny; she had dyed it a beautiful light brown and it hung down her back in a thick braid. Her makeup was flawless, as were her nails which were painted clear. You could not tell just by looking at her that she was accused of killing the most beloved politician and community activist in the black community.

By the time I entered her cell, protesters were already gathering outside of the police station demanding justice be done for the crime. They knew nothing about justice and before it was over, they would know that justice does not always come in the form of trial and jury.

Savannah remained cool as I enter her cell. I sat down and held my hand out to her. She reluctantly took it but after a while, she held onto it for dear life.

"Well, girlfriend, here we are. This ain't anything like serving on a committee is it?" she said to me with a sad smile on her face.

"Savannah, what have you done?" I replied. "Do you realize what just happened?"

"Yeah, I do. I killed a no good son of a bitch. Does that prove that I am sane?" She started to laugh before realizing that I wasn't laughing and stopped.

She leaned forward as if she felt she had to whisper to me and said, "I killed that no good, lying demon, and I don't have any regrets!"

I knew that she meant what she said. I also knew why she killed David Ban, but that knowledge was going to hurt a lot of people, and I would be one of them.

"You're going to get me out of this, Gemini Jones," she said with confidence. "And even if you don't, I won't serve a year in jail."

"Savannah, I may be good but I am no miracle worker. You could serve the rest of your life in prison," I said with tears running down my face.

"That's what I mean, Gemini, I won't serve a year. I'm dying."

Chapter 2

Hell on Earth; Home of Mamie Wells

Savannah Gill was twelve years old, pregnant, and scared. She didn't want to leave her mama and daddy; she didn't want to come to this god-awful place to have her baby. She wanted to stay at home, have the baby, and raise it. It would be just like having her very own doll that no one else could take away from her. But Nana Eva, Savannah's grandmother, said that she had to go away and have the baby. None of her daddy's church members would approve, and daddy was trying to become the superintendent for the fourth district of the Church of God Devine. So Savannah had to go away, have the baby, put it up for adoption, and return home. Nothing would be done to the man who had gotten her pregnant; Nana Eva didn't want any scandal.

Savannah entered Miss Mamie's house as the youngest girl to ever enter its doors. Her parents hadn't even bothered to see her to the door; they just let her out of the car and left, too embarrassed to see that she got inside safely. She was six months pregnant and big as a horse. She looked like a child in a third world country dying of starvation, with her poked out stomach and the fact that she was skinny as a rail didn't do her appearance much good either. Her nana had made her a couple of maternity dresses and the one that she had on was pink with white lace, which made her look like the twelve-year-old that she was, and even more pitiful. You don't expect to be sent away from home when you are twelve, and you don't expect to be pregnant either, but that was the state of affairs for little Savannah Gill.

The owner of the home was a lady (if that is what you wanted to call her) named Mamie Wells. Mamie Wells hated children but loved to sell them. She was also a frustrated drunk who was quick tempered and loved to make young girls feel even worse about themselves and their situations than they already did. She took one look at Savannah Gill and her panties became moist with pleasure. She would sell this child to some well-to-do black family and torture this little whore till she hung herself in her room like little Evelyn Woods did last year at the age of thirteen. The little whores didn't deserve to live, after what they did. Lying down on their backs, some nasty man plowing into them and having their way with them; whores, all of them, just whores! Mamie hated men too. Her husband, Usher, had run off with her younger sister, Rita, ten years earlier and had moved to Chicago. Mamie was in the last year of teachers college and had to drop out. She was devastated over what her husband and sister had done but even more so for having to drop out of school. She had bought this house and made it into a home for girls, unofficially of course. Mamie had spent the last few years torturing young mothers for their mistakes and selling their babies to black families who could provide them with a better life. Her house was not a licensed home for girls; rather she was known to have "nieces" visiting her. That she had three or four "nieces" visiting her at a time did not bother the authorities, as long as they got their share of the profits. Her lawyer saw to that and arranged all the private adoptions. That part she didn't give a damn about, she would sell a baby to the highest bidder and didn't care what happened to the baby after it left her home.

Mamie Wells was the sixth of seven children born to Seth and Etta Ruth Griggs. She was also the only dark-skinned child they had. From the very beginning, Etta made a difference between Mamie and the rest of her fair-skinned children. Seth loved his little chocolate child, she took her color after his grandmother, but Etta couldn't stand the fact that she had a dark-skinned child. After all, she was fair skinned, as was all her side of the family. Seth was not as light as she was but they had had five light-skinned children so she figured this baby would be too. But Mamie wasn't and she spent her childhood paying for something that she had no control over.

Mamie's siblings were not kind to her either. They often teased her about her dark skin and would not allow her to accompany them when they went to visit friends. Etta did nothing to defend Mamie and often had her remain home to do the household chores. Seth hated what he saw, but he said nothing.

The one thing that Mamie had that none of the other Griggs children had was brains. Mamie excelled in school and it became her salvation from the misery she suffered at home. Although the other children teased her, along with her siblings, her teachers liked the mild-mannered, quiet child who excelled in math, science, and English. She was often encouraged to participate in writing contests and science fairs and she would often place high in each contest which she participated. None of her family supported her; in fact, they often made fun of her. Once, her oldest brother Ralph spilt water on a paper that she was writing. When Mamie confronted him about it, Etta stepped in, defending Ralph, and punished Mamie.

When Mamie was fifteen years old, she became pregnant. The father was a friend of her brother, Spencer. Mamie loved the ground that Jimmy Mathis walked on and when he started paying attention to her and walking her home from school, she was in heaven. So when he asked her to go with him to the picture show in town, she accepted. Only they did not go to the movies; instead, they ended up at his home while his parents were in Indianapolis. Jimmy raped her and threatened her if she told. Mamie got home late and Etta beat her with a peach tree switch and made her go to bed without dinner.

Two months later Mamie realized that she had missed two periods and knew that she was pregnant. Not knowing what to do or who to tell, Mamie decided to take a chance and tell one of her teachers, Miss Williams. When Miss Williams heard the news, she contacted Mamie's parents and told them. Seth and Etta were very polite and acted concerned about their daughter when Miss Williams came to their home to give them the news. Etta even shed a few tears and both parents promised Miss Williams that they would look into a good girls home to send Mamie to. Once Miss Williams was gone, Etta went berserk. She called Mamie every name in the book and finally escalated into beating Mamie with a belt. When she got tired of hitting her with a belt, she resorted to hitting her with her fist. And when Mamie fell trying to get away, Etta kicked her until Mamie started to bleed. Seth said nothing but called Dr. Woods who came to the home and assisted Mamie through her miscarriage. One week after she lost the baby, Mamie was back at school, hating Miss Williams, her mother, father, siblings, and the world. The old Mamie died with the baby and a new, bitter, vindictive Mamie emerged from the damage. Life would never be the same for Mamie, her parents, or anyone who crossed her path. Two months after Mamie's miscarriage, Etta gave birth to a daughter, light skinned of course, named Rita. Mamie hated her on site.

Years later Rita would run off with Mamie's husband and bare him the children that Mamie could not. Mamie blamed children for all of the misfortune in her life.

"Come here, yella-colored whore," the head mistress yelled, "bring yo' sorry ass here."

It took Savannah several seconds to realize that the lady was talking to her, but before she could respond, she felt a pain to the right side of her face and fell to the ground. Mamie had hit her for not responding. She hit the floor with such force that the candy necklace she had in her pocket crushed into powder.

"I said come here, ya' nasty whore," Mamie screamed again. "Don't let me have ta' come afta yo' ass."

Savannah slowly got up off the floor only to be hit on the left side of her face and was sent crumbling to the ground again. Mamie was enjoying this and Savannah knew it. She just didn't know why. This time, in spite of the pain, she managed to jump up and walk toward Mamie. She did not expect the third slap across her face which sent her crumbling to the ground again. "Pick up ya' damn suitcase, whore; do you think you inna hotel or something?" Mamie was clearly enjoying the "send the whore to the floor" game. Then it occurred to her that she may do damage to the bastard that was growing inside her and decided that she had had enough for the moment. "Follow me to your room, whore," she told Savannah and led her to the room that would be hers for the next few months.

As she entered the room, Savannah could smell the Pine Sol and it made her sick to her stomach. But she knew she had better control her urge to vomit if she didn't want to get hit again. The walls of the room were papered in white with dingy flowers that were once yellow; now they were a dull dung color. The beds had worn green bedspreads on them with spots that had been sewn by hand. A brown rug barely covered the floor and the two chests of drawers had handles missing on some of the drawers. The curtains were the same dung color as the wallpaper and the only window in the room was dirty and open. Although the hot air poured into the room, the smell of Pine Sol was overpowering.

There were two beds in the room and the one by the window had a housecoat lying across it. Good, she had a roommate; someone she could talk to. It may not be so bad after all.

"Put yo' things in that closet whore and get ready to eat. Dinner is served at six p.m. every day and ya' better not miss it. The whore that shares this room with you is in the dining room. She crazy as a road lizard, but I put you in here with her. She done kick everybody else's ass in here with her crazy ass. I can't afford to have no babies born halfcocked or deformed, so I put you in here with her. She ain't gonna hit no little one like you. Bring your ass on here so that you can meet her."

Savannah and Mamie entered the dining room and the sound of laughter died down instantly. Everybody was afraid of Mamie and she knew it. Mamie looked around until her eyes spotted a young girl about fifteen sitting at the last table eating corn bread and milk. "Crazy ass, come meet yo' new roommate," Mamie said. Even she was a little afraid of the crazy girl who had beat up her help before she was subdued. The tall, lanky girl with a green dress one size too little walked slowly to the front of the room, every eye on her. She looked defiantly at the head mistress as she approached and looked down at the little girl who was to be her roommate.

"This little whore is Savannah; you better not hurt her either." The head mistress turned to Savannah and said, "This is crazy ass Gemini Jones, your roommate."

I sat there, stunned at what Savannah had just revealed to me. "Yeah, girlfriend," she continued, "I'm dying. I have breast cancer, stage four. Don't look at me like that, Gemini; say something, damn!"

"I don't know what to say, girl." The tears were beginning to flow. "What have the doctors told you, isn't there anything that can be done?"

"No, Gemini, there isn't. I waited too long to go to the doctor when I first felt the lump on my breast. I noticed that the lump got worse, but I did nothing until the pain got unbearable. I went to a female doctor who ran tests and I was diagnosed with breast cancer."

I was more devastated than she was.

"It's a very aggressive form of breast cancer. The prognosis is almost always bad. I need to have both breasts removed but I am refusing. I want to die just the way I am."

"But you don't have to die, Savannah, just have the surgery and the chemo. Come on, girlfriend, don't do this to yourself." I was trying to be cool, but it was getting harder to do.

"Listen to me, Gemini; I have had one, good, hell of a ride, despite my past and now it's time for me to leave here. I'm tired, girl; tired of fighting and hurting." I just want to go on, you know? That no good bastard took my only reason for living."

"What do you mean?"

"Gemini, David killed my daughter. He killed Gina and got away with it; until today."

I knew that was what she was going to say.

Hell on Earth; Home of Mamie Wells

Gemini looked down at the little girl and wondered, "Who da hell did this to you? He needs his ass kicked." She couldn't be any more than twelve years old, and tiny as hell. Her belly was bigger than she was.

"Are you hungry, little girl?" Gemini asked, "cause if you are, I got some food left, and you can have mine. It tastes like shit anyway." The other girls giggled at the curse word.

"You watch your cursing, Gemini;" Mamie shouted, "you know better."

"You get the hell outta my face, bitch," Gemini said back. "You know I ain't scared of you."

Mamie knew she wasn't and that made her mad as hell, but she would bide her time; she would have her way and break this crazy bitch.

"You better take care of this one. This baby is due soon and I don't want nothin' to happen to it. She gonna have her baby before you have yours."

Gemini paid no attention to Mamie, she just looked down at Savannah and said, "Let's go." And off they went to the table in the back, all eyes on the craziest girl and her young, scared, and very pregnant roommate.

Savannah's stomach was doing things and she again felt the urge to throw up but fought it as best as she could. She sat down in front of Gemini and looked at her for a *while. Gemini was not what you called pretty, she wasn't ugly either, but she had a very funny look about her. Her skin was the color of milk chocolate with long hair that just hung well past her shoulders; it was neither good nor bad, just there. Her eyes were big and shaped like the Chinese man that lived up the street from her nana. She wasn't fat but she wasn't skinny either, she just looked healthy. She had thick lips and her nose was wide like Savannah's father; Nana called it a "nigga' nose." But her face, despite the coldness, told Savannah that she had a good heart and she would look after her while she was here. This made her feel better because she was sure that the head mistress was going to mess with her until she had the baby.*

Gemini looked across the table at the girl that was going to be her roommate. Savannah was pretty; paper bag skin color, long hair past her shoulders, and pretty green eyes—cat eyes, that's what her mother called them. She had small features, hands, ears, everything about her read helpless, that's why she could not understand why somebody would want to do this to her. And where the hell was her parents, how could they let something like this happen to a little girl like her? Damn, the world was full of heartless, cruel people and they had touched the life of this young girl, all the girls in this place, including herself.

"You hungry, little girl?" Gemini asked. "You can have the rest of my food, I hate this shit."

That made Savannah giggle; she had never heard someone so young curse like that. The only time she ever heard someone curse was when she heard Nana in her room with Deacon Williams one day when no one was supposed to be home yelling, "Hell yeah, hell yeah!" She never told anybody about it but use to laugh to herself whenever she heard Nana talk about she didn't like that kind of language in her house.

"What the hell's so funny, little girl; you laughing at me?" Gemini snapped.

"I ain't ever heard a child cuss like you," Savannah replied and giggled again. She was going to like being in the room with Gemini.

"Ah, hell that isn't nothing, just wait till you see me get mad; I get mad around here all the time," Gemini replied, with her chest stuck out a little. "I get mad and cuss out Miss Wells all the time. You'll see." Gemini pushed the plate of unfinished food toward Savannah and said, "Now eat before we have to go back to our room for devotion."

"I ain't hungry, Gemini..." Then, before she could finish her statement, she felt a slap on the back of her head. It was Mamie Wells.

"Yella whore, if you don't eat the rest of that food, you better. We ain't wasting nothing 'round here. Eat; and I mean all of it."

Mamie knew that she had gone too far, but it was too late. The plate that she had demanded Savannah finish was suddenly finding its way to her face. Before she could recoil from the attack, Gemini had jumped up and pushed her down on the floor, and stood over her; eyes blazing. No one made a sound but she could hear the other girls laughing in their minds over this latest confrontation.

"Bitch, didn't she say she wasn't hungry, what part of that didn't you understand," Gemini shrieked. And with that came the two attendants, Cora and Lucy Burks, who came from inside the kitchen to help Mamie up and help subdue Gemini.

"Now, Gemini, this is between me and the yell- ah Savannah, not you."There was fear in Mamie's voice, she knew what was going on with Gemini, and it was not going to get any better until Dr. Moore came. He would give Gemini the medicine that she needed. Until then she had to remain calm. Mamie got up slowly and stood in front of Cora and Lucy who were there to protect her. She had to protect her reputation about being in control; she had to let these little whores know who was boss.

"Pick that shit up off the floor, Gemini,"Mamie said with the confidence of having two others to help her if things got bad."You know better.Who the hell do you think you are?"

"The person that's going to kick your ass and the bitches you think gonna help you," Gemini replied with the confidence of the person who had been taken off of her regular medication for the sake of the baby."That's who the hell I am. I ain't picking up nothing. Now, do you want to try to make me?" She grabbed the knife off the table and pointed it at Mamie."Or do you want to step aside and let me take my roommate back to our room."

This action with the knife scared the hell out of Cora and Lucy and they backed away. Mamie lost what confidence she had and instructed Cora and Lucy to clean up the mess that Gemini had made. Then she realized that she had not bothered to clean the mess off of her face and took the towel Cora had to use and wipe the food from her face and dress. This was a brand new dress, one that the security man hadn't seen her walk out with in the store. Now it had grease stains on it. She was going to make this crazy bitch pay. She was just going to bide her time.

"Go on to your room and take her with you,"Mamie said at last and stepped to the side for them to pass.

"Com' on, little girl," Gemini said, grabbing Savannah's hand, "let's get ready for devotion."

The odd couple walked hand in hand away to their room while the rest of the girls looked on. No one said a word; and when they were gone, Mamie turned and ordered everyone to clear the table and get ready for devotion.

"You can have the bed by the window if you want it,"Gemini told the young girl, as they entered the room. She felt so sorry for her. She was so young, stuck in this place with a fool like MamieWells, and about to become a mama."I don't mind changing with you."

"You sure?"Savannah asked. And that was the only thing she could say, the stench of the room finally got to her and she vomited all over the floor. She didn't have much in her

stomach, thank God, but the stomach juices from her stomach spilled onto the floor and the green rug. Gemini quickly grabbed one of the towels that she kept on her nightstand and quickly cleaned up the mess. Then she took some of the Pine Sol and poured it on the floor and rug. As Savannah lay down, she went out of the room and returned with the towel that she had used, dripping wet, and began to clean the floor and rug.

The smell of the Pine Sol made Savannah gag more so she ran to the window and stuck her head out. The air outside had cooled off and a breeze had filtered its way through the window. The air made her feel better after a few seconds. Gemini realized that the smell of the Pine Sol was making her sick so she left again, rinsed out the towel, and returned to try and get the smell out of the room.

"Here, let me open the window some more, maybe the breeze will get the smell out the room. I'm sorry the smell makes you sick, but Pine Sol is the only thing that bitch Wells lets us use."

By this time, Savannah was lying of the bed by the window feeling better and giggling. She liked to hear Gemini cuss; it was funny. Maybe one day she would teach her how to do it.

"Gemini, do I have time to lie down before devotion," Savannah asked; she was hoping that she had.

"About fifteen minutes or so, but we can be late," Gemini replied, placing the towel in the window to dry and returning to the bed by the door and sitting down. "But we can be late if you want. Bitch Wells isn't gonna say nothing to us. You can bet on that."

Savannah lay on the bed and giggled some more at the cuss word Gemini had just used. God had sent her an angel, an angel with a dirty mouth but that didn't matter. Hell would not be too hard to bear, now that she had Gemini to help her.

Chapter 3

If I were a drinking woman, I would have left the jail, gone straight to the liquor store, and spent the night drinking myself into a "Wesley Snipes really didn't look that bad as Noxzema Jackson" kind of drunken stupor. But I learned a long time ago that alcohol and bipolar disorder do not mix. But this was just too much for me to deal with right now. David Ban had been shot in living color, Savannah had been charged with killing him, and now she was dying. Damn, life is hard.

"Savannah, at least let me get you checked out with the prison doctor. He can prescribe some medicine for the pain; I know you're in some, aren't you?" I was trying to get her to fight; this was not the Savannah I knew. The Savannah I knew was a fighter.

"Gemini, I'm not going to take any medication, chemo, schemo, or nothing else. I want to die."

"Then why in the hell did you want me to represent you," I snapped.

"Because, if I'm going to go through hell, I want to go with God's cussing angel."

I finished my visit with Savannah, assured her that her arraignment would be soon, and left the cell. I wanted her examined by a doctor, so I arranged for her to go to the prison hospital for a checkup. I wanted to know the extent of her illness, anything I could use in her defense.

Once I arrived back at the office I sent word that I wanted to meet with my defense team ASAP. Everyone agreed that we would meet in twenty minutes. I sat down at my desk, laid my head on the back of my chair, and took a deep breath. "What the hell have you got yourself into, Gemini," I asked myself. "Will you be able to handle this? Think long and hard, sista girl; this ain't gonna be easy. They think they have Savannah dead to rights; she'll be dead before she serves a year and my career will be dead in the water if things come out about the two of us. Stop with all the dead statements. Damn, Gemini, you can be so dramatic when you want to." I did not have time to answer myself because the door came open and in walked Phillip Lyman, my investigator. "Hey, all my Gemini, what's goin' on with all of you?"

The best way to describe Phillip "Bookie" (pronounced "boo-key") Lyman is by imagining the looks of Terrance Howard and the soul of Isaac Hayes. He was not your run of the mill Lyman family member. For one, he was as light as they were dark. Two, he was as "street" as they were cultured. And three, he was as laid back as they were ambitious. The only Lyman quality Bookie had was that he was smart as hell. Bookie graduated summa cum laude from Florida A & M in Tallahassee. He had no desire to go to law school; instead, he joined a detective agency, but had to leave rather than be fired. His father decided that since Bookie needed a job and had street credibility, he would use this to the firm's advantage.

Bookie's problem was that he was quick tempered and did not like his intelligence tested. While employed at the detective agency, Bookie was hired to tail a man whose wife suspected him of cheating. The wife reported that her husband, when confronted with his infidelity, would respond by saying, "If you couldn't put your hands on me, it wasn't me!" Since the wife had no tangible proof of any wrongdoing, she sought the help of a PI, and Bookie was assigned to the case.

It took him less than a week after tailing the man to confirm what the wife already knew. What surprised Bookie was that he knew the woman that he was cheating with. She was currently Bookie's girlfriend, a stripper called Mesmerized. As Bookie approached the couple, he heard the man tell the story about his wife confronting him with their affair and him responding with "I told her if you couldn't put your hands on me, it wasn't me." Bookie tapped the man on the shoulder and as he turned around cracked him in the jaw which sent the man to the floor, and then to the hospital for surgery when the ambulance arrived. As the man hit the floor, Bookie yelled," It's you, motha' fucker, it's you!" Mesmerized, seeing what Bookie had done and realizing that he had messed with her sugar daddy, tried to attack Bookie with the knife that she kept in her bag. Bookie ducked the first attack and tried to take the knife from her. The second swing managed to rip Bookie's $500 dollar Calvin Klein jacket and his arm. To protect himself from getting stabbed a third time, Bookie delivered a sucker punch to her right jaw and she joined her sugar daddy on the floor. The police were called and Bookie was charged with assault. The charges were later dropped along with a large sum of money from Bookie's parents. Bookie resigned and came to work for his family's law firm. He was the best investigator the firm had. "I can find out if the draws Ronald Regan wears were bought by him or if they were a gift from his first wife, Jane Wyman," he once said to me. He also called me "all my Gemini" because he said he never knew who he would be talking to when he came into my office. "You know you crazy, all my Gemini, and I know it too," he joked. I normally would take offense at the name "all my Gemini" but I liked Bookie. I knew that we had mutual respect for each other and we had really become friends.

"Man, did my Uncle Quinn give you the case from hell," Bookie said as he sat down in front of my desk. "That Savannah Wooten is fine as hell; damn, what a waste."

"I do not need your negativity, Bookie, not today; not till this case is over." I know I was a little harsh but I was tense and Bookie knew me well enough to take it in stride, but take it seriously.

"Okay, okay, all my Gemini, all y'all just take it easy. I'll be cool for this; don't worry."

"And where the hell is everybody else? I said twenty minutes." I was feeling the pressure of this case and I did not like what was going on.

"All my Gemini, just be cool babe, they are coming. It has only been five minutes. I just wanted to come in and give all you your pep talk; I know all you need one right now. Hey, you know if my Uncle Quinn assigned this case to you he has the confidence that you're gonna make this firm come out smelling like a rose."

"Oh, so you don't think that I can provide the best defense for my client, is that what you and the firm think about me?" I snapped, "Gemini, where in the hell is all this coming from?" I asked myself.

"All my Gemini, now you really are being crazy. You know what they say about you, 'If you kill a man in Times Square at noon in front of ten thousand people, Gemini Jones is the lawyer to get.' Savannah Wooten got the best, babe; the best money can buy and God could send. I wished that I had had you when I knocked the shit outta my girl and her friend. I would have considered catching a case on them!" This made me laugh; Bookie knew how to make me laugh.

"Shut up, Bookie, you don't have the sense you were born with." Just then, the rest of my team came in for what would turn out to be a brain storming session.

When Quinn Lyman told me that I would have the best the firm had to offer, he was right. I felt like Mr. Phelps on the old Mission Impossible show; I had the cream of the crop for a mission that seemed impossible, defending Savannah Wooten.

Antoinette Clark-Flowers would be my legal secretary and Bookie, my investigator. My paralegals looked like the rainbow coalition, Israel Feldman, Suni Hso, Malcolm George, and Rosita Alba. Jewish, Chinese, black, and Latino, we would need every damn body to get this done.

"Gemini, what is this? No 'we gonna be here all damn day feast?'" It was Israel making his usual incoming joke, he could never just walk in a room and sit down; he always had something to say. He was well liked in the firm. Not only because he was funny and likeable but also because he was as smart as, if not smarter than, Bookie and the firm was lucky to have him. Behind him came Malcolm. He is very quiet, I really don't think he will be here long; he has ambitions and a hidden agenda. He's not bad looking; dark-skinned brotha with distinct African features, broad nose, thick lips, and very course hair, which he wears short. A brotha that any sista would be happy to hang on to. Suni came in next. She is taller than most Chinese people that I have seen, and beautiful. She has long black hair, which she has braided in one long braid that hung down to her waist. Suni appears to be soft spoken, but she was very outspoken and sharp as a whip; her research skills were the best that I had ever seen. I would like to have taken her under my wing, but one of the partners had beaten me to the punch. She would make a great attorney and I wanted to encourage her to go to law school. The last person to arrive was Rosita. I don't know what criteria the firm had as far as its hiring practice goes, but one thing you had to be was attractive, as well as smart. Rosita was that for sure. Short, petite, beautiful olive skin, and dark brown hair, which she wore to her shoulders. Rosita was also a fireball; quick tempered, quick witted, and sharp as a whip. She and Israel often got into matches with each other pitting wit against wit. The whole office would be cracking up with laughter when those two went at it.

"Well, as Bugs Bunny would say, "Hush my mouth and call me corn pone," Antoinette said as everyone came in and took a seat, "the crème de la crème has arrived." Antoinette is known for her silly sayings and is always quoting of all well-known celebrities, Bugs Bunny.

"We know who has a major influence in your life," Bookie said in response to Antoinette's Bugs Bunny statement. "Daffy Duck and Porky Pig would be proud."

"What a maroon," Antoinette snapped back.

"You mean moron, don't you?" said Bookie. "Oh, I know Bugs Bunny again. Next you'll be quoting Speedy Gonzales."

"Hey! What's wrong with Speedy?" Rosita chimed in. "That mouse is making money."

"Yeah," said Antoinette, "but Bugs is the man and has money up the whazoo. And he shared it with Daffy, Porky, Sylvester, Tweedy, Foghorn Leghorn..."

"That's my rooster, Foghorn," I said.

"Foghorn Leghorn," Bookie shot back, imitating the cartoon character which sent everyone into laughter. I was not in the mood.

"Would you like me to have a color TV brought in so you can catch cartoons?" I snapped. I knew I was losing it, but it had been a long day and my brain was tired. It got quiet in the room before Bookie said, "Gem, I say, Gemini, I do believe you are angry." That sent everyone into laughter again. I sat there mad as hell for a second then realized how silly I was acting and started to laugh myself. Thank God for Bookie.

"O, I say okay, everyone, let's cut this shit out and get started!" My foghorn Leghorn imitation made everyone laugh even more. The laughter started to die down in a few seconds and the meeting began.

"Okay, as you know we have a case ahead of us that is going to make or break us," I started out saying. "I am just waiting to hear from the DA's office about the charges, but I would guess murder one."

"The DA's office called just before I came in," Antoinette said. "Guess who has the case? None other than Ms. Amanda Thornburg Simmons! The ice queen called! Her high ass, err, highness wants to meet with you tomorrow in her office before the arraignment. She probably figures that you will want to try to plea bargain."

"I want to talk with Savannah again and let her decide. If we can plea, we will. But I think Amanda wants me to beg so that she can say no, hell no!" I turned to Malcolm. "I want the scoop on who the police are interviewing, and I want to know about every news story out there."

"Not a problem, my lady," Malcolm said. "I'm on it."

"Suni, I want you to research breast cancer. Savannah has been diagnosed with it. See how it affects the mind."

"Are you going with an insanity plea, Gemini?" Israel asked.

"I don't know yet, but I want to cover all my bases. Antoinette, I will need the medical examiner's report on Ban. And set up a meeting with Amanda Thornburg-Simmons tomorrow after I have had a chance to talk with Savannah again. Let's make it at eleven a.m." I gave the rest of them their assignments.

"Will do, your lawyerness." Antoinette was always coming up with a silly little name for me.

"Listen up, everyone; get ready to work harder than you have ever worked in your life. I am going to try to save Savannah's life and I am going to need all the help that I can get. I am counting on each and every one of you to pull this off. If you don't think that you have what it takes to keep up with me, let me know now. I won't hold it against you." The room remained quiet. "Okay, I continued, let's get started and save Savannah's life. Let's meet in a couple of days. I may even call an impromptu meeting if the need arises. Okay, if no one has any questions, I will see you later. Bookie, will you and Antoinette stay on a second?"

The others left and as Antoinette closed the door for them, Bookie turned to me and said, "All right, all my Gemini, what's up with Savannah Wooten and David Ban?"

I told them the story of what happened to Savannah when she was twelve years old and told Bookie what I wanted him to find out. For the first time since I have known him, Phillip Bookie Lyman was speechless.

"And you want me to find out if it is true?"

"I know it's true."

"Well, you want me to find out what happened to the daughter."

"I know what happened to her daughter, she died."

"And you want me to find out who she was."

"No, I want you to find out if David Ban killed her."

"Is that Savannah's motive for shooting him, besides raping her?"

"Ain't that enough?"

I left the office at seven p.m. and went straight home. Kyrra, my "lil' ho" dog, is in heat and when I opened the door, she tried to run out to do her "thang." But I was faster than she was, and put her down in the basement where she would be safe from all the males that were circling the block. As I put her in the basement, I felt sorry for her. Here she just wanted to do what she does naturally and I was "blocking." Antoinette told me I was just jealous because Kyrra was getting some and I wasn't.

Once, a dog had even slipped into my back door and I caught them doing their thing in the middle of my living room. I screamed for my neighbor who came running over and doubled over in laughter when he saw the lovers in the middle of my living room stuck together. The only thing we could do was wait for my lil' ho' dog, a lab and German shepherd mix, and the black lab, known in the hood as "Zen", to finish their business. When they did, Zen fled out the front door that my neighbor had left opened.

I fixed myself a light salad, picked at it, and finished a two liter bottle of diet Pepsi. There was nothing on TV that interested me, so I just sat on my couch and stared at the ceiling. I knew that I had work to do, I had to figure out what I was going to do to come up with a reasonable defense for Savannah, but I was feeling overwhelmed over the whole thing and I was tired. Being tired is not a good thing when you are bipolar. I knew that it was time to call my doctor and let her know what was going on.

Dr. Elmonda Gray has been my doctor for the past few years. I found her shortly after I went to work for the public defender's office. I am one of the few patients that have her home and cell phone number. We have a great relationship, although it has never gone beyond doctor/patient.

I dialed her number and got her on the second ring. I could hear the sound of jazz playing in the background and I knew she was not alone. She always played jazz when she had company.

"Hello, Gemini, I have been trying to reach you. How is the new medication that I prescribed?"

"Hey, you're playing jazz, that means that a fine ass brotha, tall, dark handsome, and rich, is making dinner for you or you're about to serve him dessert." I realized what I said after I said it and felt stupid.

"Gemini, you're avoiding my question. Are you taking the new medication?"

I told her the truth; that I had skipped a couple of days because I had been so busy, but that I was going to take a dose before I went to bed. I also told her about representing Savannah and that the case could expose the skeletons in her and my past.

"Gemini, I don't have to tell you how important taking your medication is, especially now. Which brings me to my next question; why did you agree to take the case?"

"Because Savannah asked for me and the firm feels that I can handle it."

"The question is whether you feel you are able to handle the case."

"I have to handle it."

"Do they know that the two of you have history?"

"Not all the history that we have. They know that she and I have worked on several charitable committees together. That's all."

"Again, why did you agree to take the case?" Elmonda was trying to get me to come to some conclusion, but I did not know what it was.

"I told you, the firm feels that I can do it and Savannah needs me"

"And what about you, what do you need? Do you think that you can deal with what may or may not come out in this trial?"

"I don't know; I just know that Savannah needs me. And I want to do this."

"Well, if you want to do this then don't you think that you need to let the firm know the whole story about the two of you?'"

"I know, I do, but part of me is not ready to reveal that part of my life to anyone outside of family and you. And what if they give the case to someone else? No one is going to treat Savannah like I will. And besides, she trusts me."

"Then I guess you have made up your mind. But you do need to talk with Quinn when you go in tomorrow morning. I think you may be surprised at what he has to say."

"Yeah, I think that you are right. I think part of my anxiety is the fact that I have not been completely honest with him."

"Good, I know that you are doing the right thing, like taking your medication like you're supposed to."

"I will, I promise."

"Call my office tomorrow and make an appointment."

"I'll have Antoinette give your office a call first thing in the morning." I hung up knowing I had lied.

Chapter 4

Hell on Earth; Home of Mamie Wells

Savannah and Gemini settled into a routine at the home for girls. They were usually out of bed by 6:00 a.m., showered, dressed, and at breakfast by 6:30. Savannah was still having trouble holding her food, and she was so afraid to eat, but Gemini made her eat anyway. Gemini had no problems eating anything; in fact, she would usually bully the other girls to give up their toast or a slice of bacon.

After breakfast, the girls usually went to devotion. Devotion was usually held in the main sitting room where the girls would sit and listen to Rev. Charles Granger say some encouraging words about straightening out their lives once they returned home. He was the pastor of the local black Baptist church in the city and a well-respected man. Only Gemini knew his real reason for coming here every day. He usually supplied the couples who wanted to "adopt" the babies when they were born and got a nice kickback for his services. He was also screwing the hell out of Lucy and Cora. There were times when Gemini couldn't sleep and would walk the halls. One night, during one of her walks, she happened to see the good reverend slip out of the devotional room with Cora. They were both straightening their clothes and did not see her. Two weeks later, on another one of her walks, she saw the good reverend coming out of the devotional room with Lucy. Neither one knew he was sleeping with the other. Gemini decided that she would keep this information to herself until the time was right.

After devotion, there were chores, depending on how far along you were. Gemini was sent to the kitchen because she was only five months pregnant and could still lift the dishes once they were washed. If she got tired, she would sit and peel potatoes, shuck peas, or pick greens. Savannah, who was in her seventh month, was sent to the nursery to help with the newborns. She was taught how to hold the babies, change their diapers, and rock them when they cried. Once the mother gave birth, she was not allowed to see her baby. The baby was placed in the nursery to await the adoptive parents to show up and take them home.

Savannah worried as her time approached about giving birth. She had heard from some of the other girls that having babies was painful and that was something she dreaded. Plus, she wanted to keep her baby; she didn't want any strangers taking her baby. But Nana had put her foot down and said that the baby had to go to another family. Gemini told her that even though she would probably never see her baby, it would more than likely go to a rich black family and the baby would be well taken care of.

But none of that was comforting to Savannah. She wanted to keep her baby. She wanted to hold it and rock it just like she did the babies in the nurseries. She had milk in her chest just for the baby and she knew how to feed the baby cause that is one of the things that she did in the nursery. The thought of not seeing her baby once it was born made the tears that she promised Gemini she would not shed come down like a waterfall.

She also worried about Gemini. One minute she was upbeat and very talkative, and then silent the next. She did not understand what was going on with her friend. Sometimes Gemini would lie in her bed and cry for no reason, and then be up talking about beating the shit out of Bitch Wells the next. Gemini really was crazy. But she was her friend and protector, so she could be as crazy as she wanted to be.

Mamie, who had come in to inspect "her bounty," saw the tears on Savannah's face and started in on her immediately. "What the hell's wrong with you, yella ho?" By that time Mamie had made her way to Savannah and was standing over her. The slap across Savannah's face left a red mark on her skin. "Stop that damn crying, ho. You got yourself in this mess, now you going to have to face the music. You wanna keep your baby but you ain't, it's going to go to a home where there aren't any hoes like you and it's going to be raised by a family with money and it will have a life better than you will ever have. You will never amount to nothing! You are spoiled goods and God ain't gonna let nothing good happen to you 'cause you are spoiled goods."

"And what does that make you, bitch?" Mamie and Savannah turned around to see Gemini standing in the doorway. "You ain't amounted to nothing either, just a black ass bitch who sells babies to the people with the most money. I read in my history books that that is called slavery."

"Get the hell out of here, Gemini, this does not have anything to do with you," Mamie replied, her voice shaking. She was really scared of this crazy girl.

"This has everything to do with me, she is my roommate and I am supposed to protect her and show her the ropes. Ain't that what you said?" Gemini was standing in Mamie's *face and ready to beat the shit out of her, five months pregnant or not. For seconds the two faced off with Gemini praying to the all mighty that Mamie would hit or push her. Mamie did not move. The look in her eyes told Gemini that she was afraid. It paid sometimes to be crazy and have a history of violence.*

Mamie backed away and Gemini took Savannah's hand and walked out of the room. As the two walked out of the room, Mamie called Gemini a bitch under her breath. One day she would get that crazy ho; one day Gemini would wish she was dead and Mamie would give her her wish.

"Didn't I tell you not to be crying around that crazy bitch?" Gemini snapped as she and Savannah made their way back to their room. "I told you she just waiting to get you."

"I'm soooo sorreeeeee, Gemini," Savannah cried, "I can't help it. They gonna take my baby when it's born and I will never see her again." The tears were more than even hard ass Gemini could take. It made her angry.

"Stop that crying right now." She grabbed Savannah and forced her to face her. "Stop it right now; there ain't nothing you can do about it. Who told you to open your legs and get this baby? Now you have to live with it!" Gemini hated to say what she just said, but Savannah was crying so hard and she was powerless to help her.

"But I didn't lie down and get this baby, not by myself," Savannah responded. "He made me do this. I did not want to do it. It hurt too."

Gemini didn't know why she was so startled at what Savannah had said, of course she was raped. She was only twelve years old; she didn't know anything about having sex. She was just a baby herself. Gemini had been raped also, but she was fifteen at the time and able to fight back. Savannah hadn't had a chance.

"Look, stop crying right now and lay down for a while." They were both back in the room, which was cooler now that Gemini had the fan her parents had sent her. "We will talk when you wake up. Maybe we can find a way for you to keep the baby. I know; we will write your nana a letter telling her how much you want this baby."

"You'll do that for me, Gemini?" Savannah said through tear-drenched eyes.

"I ain't making any promises; she might say no."

"But at least somebody tried to help me," Savannah said at last, the weariness apparent in her voice.

"Yeah, but if you don't learn to control your crying around Mamie, I ain't gonna lift a finger to help you." Gemini didn't mean what she just said; she only wanted to stop Savannah from crying so much.

"Okay, Gemini, I'll try, but it ain't easy. Sometimes I just can't control myself, something in my body makes me cry sometimes."

"I know; it's called hormones, they do stupid stuff to women."

"Gemini, thank you for helping me. I get scared sometimes, I can't help. It..."
Savannah was asleep before Gemini could say "you're welcome."

I did not sleep well that night; taking my medication would have helped. There were so many things were going through my mind, Savannah, her child, David Ban, his death, and my own demons. I tried the warm milk thing my mother used on me when I was a child, but that didn't work. So I watched an old movie on the Late Late Show, *Double Indemnity* with Fred MacMurray and Barbara Stanwyck. I love that movie, I have watched it over and over again, and I always hope that Fred MacMurray will change his mind and decide not to help Barbara kill her husband. But once they do, I find myself hoping that they will get away with it, but Edward G. Robinson always figures it out. In the old movies, the killer never gets away with crime. I thought about Savannah and the trouble that she had gotten herself, and me, into. I would have to tell Quinn about it when I met with him early the next morning.

How was I going to tell Quinn that Savannah and I were in a home for girls together when she was twelve and I was fifteen and both of us were pregnant? I had not thought about that time in my life for a lifetime and now Savannah was bringing it all back, and according to witnesses, in living color. I was nervous about meeting with Quinn because I had not been completely honest with him. I wouldn't be surprised if he took me off the case, but I wanted to stay on this case; I wanted to fight for Savannah, she deserved that after all the mess that happened to her in her life. She had managed to make something of herself despite the early horrors she experienced as a child.

I was still awake when the news came on again from the previous night. I decided to get up and start planning my agenda for the meeting with the district attorney after my meeting with Quinn. Then I realized that I might not have to have that meeting with her. Once Quinn found out about my past with Savannah, he might assign the case to another attorney. He may even take the case himself. I am surprised that he hadn't taken the case; it was the case that attorneys like Quinn live for. He has never lost a case and is one of the most respected lawyers in the city, if not the state. He has turned down two cabinet jobs in Washington, as well as turning down the chance to run for lieutenant governor for the state. Quinn really likes what he does.

I worked for several hours for my meeting with the ADA, and at five, I jumped in the shower. I looked for something to wear, finally settling for a Jones of New York navy blue suit and a light blue Calvin Klein blouse. I had purchased some new shoes from black designer Lakota Truman and custom jewelry from Rings and Things, where Bookie had a share in the business. Rings and Things was doing well, it is a boutique and they have clothes, shoes, purses, fragrances, you name it from all the top black designers.

By 7:00 p.m., I was out the door and heading for my new Audi that I had purchased for my last birthday. I arrived at the office and after putting my things away, made my way up the hall to the suite of Quinn Lyman.

I opened the two huge cherry wood doors, and entered the receptionist area where I was greeted by his receptionist and niece, Lydia Lyman. Lydia was still trying to find herself. She had gotten into some problems when she was younger and was now trying to get her life in order. Uncle Quinn had given her a job as a receptionist, despite the objections from her father, Donald, and her mother, Trina Lyman. Donald Webber, Quinn's childhood friend, was a partner in the firm, along with Marshal Strain who was also a longtime friend to Quinn and Donald from high school. They had all attended high school together, had gone to Vietnam at the same time, and had all returned to the community after they got out of the service. Quinn was the first one to go to school, followed by Marshall, and finally Donald joined the group. They were known at Texas Southern as the men with vision because they knew from the start that they wanted to practice law, and practice it together. After graduating from Thurgood Marshall School of Law, the three started their practice in the back of Sammie John's barbershop in the hood.

They started out defending small time pushers, hookers, petty thieves, and the occasional pimp. What was amazing about them was that they seldom lost a case. The more they won, the more popular they became; and the clients began to come in who had money, money, and more money. Ten years later, they were the number one black law firm in the city; and five years later, the number one black law firm in the state.

Quinn wanted to be updated on Savannah's case daily and I was pretty sure he wanted to keep abreast on my health as well. After all, this case was riding on how well of a defense I could come up with and how well I held up.

Lydia looked up at me when I entered and smiled. "Nice to see you, Miss Gemini. Uncle Quinn said to go right in when you get here." Lydia was not what you call a pretty girl, but she had a beautiful smile and great personality and that would take her a long way.

"Thanks, Lydia," I said and walked past her into Quinn's office.

You can tell the sign of success when you enter Quinn Lyman's office. The redwood desk and accessories grab your eye the minute you walk into the room. The black leather couch and matching chairs form a sitting room at the front of the office and the big desk where Quinn was sitting when I walked in was handmade in Africa and purchased by the woman in Quinn's life, but no one knew who that was at the moment. She just continued to make her presence known by the way she was decorating his office. Quinn was sitting in the Corinthian leather chair his new lady friend had picked out for him; behind him was a picture of Quinn and Miles Davis standing side by side. The picture was taken years ago in Chicago. Miles Davis and Quinn had become friends and Miles agreed to pose with Quinn for the picture. The original eight by ten sat on the table to the left of Quinn along with pictures of the rest of his family, but the new lady had had the picture blown up and it was placed on the wall behind Quinn's desk.

He looked up at me as I entered and sat down. He looked tired but his eyes were still just as alert as they always were. His eyes were his best feature; they were light brown, almost amber in color. His sandy brown hair was cut short and he was balding in the front, female pattern baldness obviously ran in the family. Quinn was 6 foot three and weighed well over 275, but he worked out a lot so he was solid. He had big hands with long slender fingers, which made sense since he was a very accomplished jazz pianist. His clothes were all tailored made and he wore them well. He played basketball, tennis, golf and I also knew that he swam at least ten laps a day.

"Gemini, have a seat. So are you ready to meet with the ADA this morning? If so, what will be your defense?"

"Quinn, I am ready, but before I tell you my strategy, there is something I need to tell you so that there won't be any secrets between us."

"Is this about your relationship with Savannah Wooten," he asked, but he already knew the answer.

"Yes, it is. I should have said something to you about it when you first asked me to take the case, but I thought it wouldn't matter until I met with Savannah yesterday. Now I am not so sure."

"I take it you two have more history together than you have let on, is that it?"
"Yes."

"Does this history have the potential to keep you from giving her the best defense?"

"No."

"Will this history bring unwelcomed bad press to the firm? Not that we aren't use to that, I just need to know how to proceed if it does."

"It might."

"Then you had better tell me what it is." And I did, I told him the whole story from beginning to end. Quinn sat quietly while I spilt my guts about me, Savannah, our past, her child, and David Ban's role in all of it. After I finished I felt as if I had been through a boxing match but, surprisingly, I felt relieved.

Quinn sat there for a while, I think out of shock, not for Savannah and I but for what he had heard about David Ban. He had been a staunch supporter of Ban and if Quinn Lyman backed you, then you had to be on the up and up. Quinn never backed losers.

"Gemini, I wish you had told me this from the very beginning, not that it would have made any difference, I still want you on the case, but it would have been nice to know. There might be some recourse to pay from all of this. I am also a bit shocked to hear about David, it makes sense now why he appeared to be so protective of his family and fought so hard to keep his private life just that, private. Gemini, I really think you can handle this case, even after what I have just heard. But we are going to have to do a lot of investigation into David's past and that could get ugly. Are you prepared for that?"

"The life of David Ban is going to be my defense. It is about time people realized who he was and what he did. A lot of people are going to be upset, but after the facts come out, I have a feeling we will have a good chance of winning."

"If that is what you think, then go for it, Gemini, just make sure that Bookie knows what to look for and where to look. First of which is to find out what the DA has on the case. Do they have enough to go on? The fact that the DA wants to meet with you so early tells me things are quite well for the DA. You should find out soon enough. Well, keep me posted and if you need anything, I mean anything, do not hesitate to let me know. I want you to succeed for yourself, your client, and the firm. But I would like to bask in the comfort that we can beat the DA. Close the door for me on your way out." And with that I promptly got up, walked out the door past Lydia, and finally down the hallway to where Bookie was waiting for me, just like a mother hen!

"Hey, all my Gemini, how are we doing today? Are we ready for our visit with the ADA? And who am I talking with today, Gemini? Is it you or one of your personalities, you know you got at least six different ones inside you! Smile, baby girl, it is a day to behold!"

Sometimes I wanted to poison Bookie, slowly. But today was just not one of those days. I wanted to sit with him and listen to what he had come up with, if anything, on the shooting, what the press was making of it, and what the word was at the city jail and the courts.

Bookie walked with me down to my office and as we walked in, one of the paralegals assigned to me, Israel Feldman, was talking nonstop to Antoinette, my secretary. The excitement on his face told me that he had found something out early in the game and was eager to share his knowledge.

"Everybody in my office, now. And, Antoinette, tell the others to join us also," I said and the four of us walked in. I sat at my desk while Antoinette, Bookie, and Israel stood around me. I gave Bookie the first shot since he was the first one I ran into. Suni, Malcolm, and Rosita walked in just as Bookie was about to speak.

"Word is that Savannah and Ban were having an affair, and that Ban told her it was off. Apparently, the wife knew nothing of it and invited Ms. Wooten to the press conference. Now, here's the part that's gonna knock your socks off. None of the film actually shows Savannah shooting Ban. All the cameras were on Ban when the shots rang out. By the time the cameras were on her, the gun was already at her feet!"

"Then what do they have on her?" I asked, suddenly feeling better about this case than I had a moment before.

"Her fingerprints were on the gun and it is registered in her name," Bookie replied. "And she has never said that she did not shoot him, on the contrary, she said she did."

"But," chimed in Israel, "there was no gun residue on her hands! But we do know that her gun was the murder weapon."

"What else do you have?" I asked. "This may be a good day after all."

"So far that is all I have," said Bookie.

Israel spoke up, "Ban and his wife were talking divorce, but not until after the election. He wanted to make sure he got elected first before he let her go. So, he may have been having an affair with someone, we just don't know who. Rumor has it that he was still grieving the death of his sister, Gina Ban. She killed herself."

I winced when Israel made that statement, one out of my pain over Gina killing herself; and two over the fact that I knew what would have been the reason Savannah would have shot Ban. I was going to be late for my meeting with the ADA, so I excused everyone and asked Antoinette to call a taxi for me. It would be better for me to taxi over. That would give me more time to get my thoughts together.

It was Malcolm's turn to speak. "The witnesses that they have are a joke. Mr. Benjamin Isaac, who claims that he saw Savannah drop the gun, has already tried to sell his story to the newspapers and to Fox News. And the story has changed from 'I saw her drop the gun' to 'I saw her shoot Ban and then drop the gun.' The other witness, Dora Jefferson, has left town and no one, including the police, know where she is." That bit of information would help me when I went to meet with the ADA. Things were beginning to look up!

Chapter 5

I was meeting ADA Thornburg-Simmons at her office. I agreed so that we could discuss the case at length because she was going to be in meetings all day. The prosecutor's office building is new and the envy of the town. It is black steel and glass and stands fourteen stories in the air. The DA's office was on the top floor and rumor had it that he had half of the floor as his office space; the other half was going to be used for press conferences and other media events.

The ADA offices were located on the fourth floor and were crap compared to DA Robinson's office. Simmons's secretary led me to the conference where I had to wait twenty minutes for her to arrive.

I had never met Amanda Thornburg Simmons, but I felt an instant dislike for her when she walked through the door. Tall, blond, and tanned, she looked like Barbie home from the beach, right down to the little turned up nose she had between the coldest pair of dark blue eyes I had ever seen. She reeked of being rich, spoiled, and pampered; your typical, stuck up rich girl. Boy was I wrong, the minute she opened her mouth, all I heard was Midwest blue collar.

"Damn, I hate these damn panties hose. The damn DA wants us to wear them all the damn time. I didn't wear shoes until I went to school. Hell, I even took them off then! Hi there, I'm Amanda and you must be Gemini. Damn, I heard a lot about you." She had the thickest Chicago accent I had ever heard in my life. I was floored and amazed at the same time.

"Nice to meet you, Amanda," I replied. I really did not know how to take her and obviously I would have a hard time sizing her up. We shook hands and as she sat down, she started talking a million miles per minute.

"Let me be frank with you, I have a good case and we could ask for life without parole. But I am willing to go with murder two, in which case she will get a max of twenty-five years."

"What do you have that makes you so sure you can win the case?" I felt that there was something that she was not going to tell me, but I could see that she was pretty confident about making this case.

"We have the gun registered to her, fingerprints on the gun belong to her, and she has not one time professed her innocence."

"That's funny," I replied, "my sources tell me that no TV station has actual footage of the crime. What else do you have?"

"What else do we need? We have her written statement."

"Which the police got without reading her her rights. What else do you have?"

"Oh, I don't know, an eyewitness or two or three, motive, you know all the things that dream cases are made of. We have two eyewitnesses and the motive is he dumped her after their affair ended. Ah, yes, and we have her confession. What do you think about that?" She was really confident about this one.

"Tell me about the two witnesses."

"One is a Mr. Benjamin Isaac. Mr. Isaac was standing in front of the audience and will swear that he saw your client drop the gun."

"And the other witness?"

"Dora Jefferson! She will testify that she too was looking right at Ms. Wooten when she fired the gun and that she ran up to try and stop her from shooting again and that Savannah dropped the gun by the time the police had arrived."

"Then why is there no gun powder residue on her hands? Can you explain that?"

"Yes, we can, and we will."

"Do you care to explain it to me now?"

"Damn, Gemini, you know damn well that just because a gun has been fired, that does not mean there will be powder residue. Shoot, honey, I know you know this."

"Amanda, can I shoot straight from the hip? Sorry, no pun intended. You don't have jack shit. You got two people who claimed to have seen my client shoot David Ban, one who claims she tried to get the gun away from her. Who in their right mind would try to take a gun away from someone and they are not armed themselves? And now I hear that you don't have a clue where she is right now, she has apparently left town. Your other witness has already tried to sell his story to the media, and the story has changed I've been told. I cannot wait to get them both on the stand, that is, if you can find Dora Jefferson." The look on her face made me realize that I had made an impression. "Secondly, for her to be so close to Ban and the way that he was shot, there would be gun residue on her hands and her suit, yet your office claims that there was no powder residue on her hands. That is bullshit and you know it."

"Well, we still have her confession, and that will take this case a long way!" By this time she was looking at me as if to say, "I got your poor, bipolar ass in a sling, black chile', and don't you forget it!"

"Which I am sure I can have thrown out. You got jack shit! I am surprised that DA Robinson is letting you try this case. I just knew this case would be the one he would select to get him into the governor's office."

"Didn't I tell you that I am second chair? DA Robinson is going to try this case."

That only meant one thing; he had something up his sleeve that would prove detrimental to my client. I had to find out what he knew.

"So your plea bargaining is on behalf of gover… err, I mean DA Robinson?"

"You don't want to mess with him, do you, Gemini? Were you born under that sign by the way?"

"Yes, I do, and no I was not."

"So you won't take the bargain? Twenty-five years ain't so long; David Ban is dead forever."

"What about second degree manslaughter, six to nine years? And my client might be dead forever soon also. She has breast cancer and does not want treatment."

"Well, Gemini, I think I'll just let the good DA know and we will get back with you."

"He won't go for that and you know it, but I will wait for your call!" I got up, shook hands with "attorney Barbie," and left. As I left the office, I yelled over my shoulder, "See you at the arraignment."

I stopped by the jail to see Savannah and was told by the guard that she was taken to Community Hospital because she was spitting up blood. I asked why I was not called and the guard explained that they only contact next of kin and that Savannah had not put anyone down on the form. I arrived at the hospital, went to Savannah's room, and identified myself to the guard stationed at her door as her attorney. She looked worse today than she did the day before. I noticed that she had her eyes closed and she appeared to be mouthing something, it was only when I got closer that I realized she was praying. I said nothing but watched her and when she finished, she must have sensed my presence because she opened her eyes and a little sparkle of recognition and gratitude crossed her face.

"Hey, girlfriend, how you holding up today?" I said as I held her hand. It was cold and clammy at the same time.

"I am blessed, Gemini. You look like shit!

"I'm fine; but it is not about me, it's about you."

"I am going to join my baby soon."

"Not if I can help it, I want you to at least consider chemo."

"I am at stage four of this disease, Gemini, and I am not going to prolong this."

"At least tell me what happened on that day, I have not heard the story from you and I need to know what happened."

"Gemini, it is not hard to figure out. I killed him because he killed my baby!"

"But not one TV station out there that day got you on tape killing me; let alone killing David. Just when did you have time to do it?

"I should have done it when I was eleven, but I couldn't. We would all have been better off."

Chapter 6

Savannah's Baby is Born; Home of Mamie Wells

Savannah woke up with the worst pain she had ever felt in her life. She woke screaming and holding her stomach. Was this labor; was it time to have her baby? By the time she got through thinking about her situation, another wave of pain came over her. This time the scream she let out woke Gemini up with a startle.

"Oh damn, Savannah, why the hell are you yelling?" Then it dawned on her what was going on.

"Oooh shit, is it time to have the baby?" Gemini was out the bed and at Savannah's side within seconds. "Hold on tight, little girl, I will go get Bitch Wells.

"Please don't leave me, Gemini," Savannah yelled. "I'm scared; can't you just wake Norma up next door and tell her to get Mrs. Wells?"

"Hell naw, just hold on and I will run and get her myself." With that, Gemini ran out the door and down the hall to Mamie's door. She knocked and told Mamie what was going on.

"Run get Cora and Lucy and tell them to call the doctor and come to the room ASAP!"

"ASAP?" Gemini didn't know what that meant. Mamie spat back rather vehemently, "As soon as possible, dumb ass! Tell them to call the doctor and come as soon as possible."

Gemini was out the door and down the hall before she realized what Bitch Wells had just said to her. She would not forget and would make the bitch suffer for that remark.

Mamie entered Gemini and Savannah's room and heard Savannah crying as she approached the bed.

"Don't worry, lil ho, it will all be over with soon. The doctor will be here and we gonna put you to sleep and take that baby off your hands. Then when you wake up it will all be over with and in a few days you can go back to your momma and daddy and live like whores like you do. I got me a nice family want to take your baby and raise it and they are willing to pay big money!"

Savannah wasn't listening; she was in pain, and wanted it over with. Cora and Lorna arrived and by the time Gemini entered the room, the three women had Savannah up and walking toward the door. She looked scared and it broke Gemini's heart to see her suffer like that. She wanted to be with her and said so to Mamie.

"Well that ain't happening, the doctor won't let you. Besides, she got the three of us so don't you worry about nothing. Just stay here and I will let you know what she has."

That was that and the four of them were gone.

The doctor met the four by the door of the birthing room. He got them to put Savannah in bed and remove her clothes from the waist down so that he could examine her. She had dilated but he felt compelled to give her a C-section since she was so small, and thought he had time to do so. He was wrong. As he was conducting his exam, he noticed that the head had already started to come out. So he positioned himself at the foot of the bed and told Savannah to push. He thought her rather brave because she did as she was told and after a few minutes, the baby had come completely out and needed no assistance in crying; she was yelling for dear life.

"It's a girl," the doctor told Mamie, "and mother is doing fine!"

Mamie took the child from the doctor, looked at the little pale baby in her arms, and thought, "This child is so light skinned I can double my price. And look at the head full of good hair she has. She just like her daddy."

Yes, Mamie knew who the father was and who was going to pay big money for this child.

The baby's birth had torn Savannah so she was given a sedative while the doctor stitched her up. She was then left in the birthing room for the evening. She never got to see her baby that night.

Gemini had witnessed the whole thing and saw Mamie take the baby to the nursery. She waited until everyone was out of the birthing room and snuck in to see Savannah. Poor thing, she was sound asleep and looked so peaceful. Gemini sat beside her for about an hour and then decided to go back to her room and wait until the next day to see her.

The next morning when Savannah awoke, the first thing she asked for was to see her baby. Cora, who was with her at the time, said it would not be a good idea because she might get attached to the baby which made Savannah cry. She was still crying an hour later when Gemini came in to see her.

"Savannah, what's the matter? You okay?"

"They won't let me see my baby, Gemini. Why can't I see my baby?"

"Get up, I know where your baby is and I will take you to her."

"Her? You mean I had a girl!"

"Yep, and she is as pretty as can be. I snuck in the nursery to look at her. She's the only one in there now and she is so pretty; she reminds me of you."

"Please take me to her."

So Gemini helped Savannah up and together they snuck down the hall to the nursery so that Savannah could see her child. As they entered the nursery, they could hear the baby crying, and when Savannah saw her baby for the first time, she gasped. She had never seen anything so beautiful in her life. Someone had dressed her baby in a pink dress and pink socks to match. One of Cora's crocheted baby hats sat on her head, which, when Savannah lifted it, revealed a head full of soft curly hair. Her eyes were light brown and she had the cutest little round face any baby could have. Savannah cried as she held her daughter.

"Gemini, what am I going to do? I want my baby, I know I'm a baby myself but I want my baby. What can I do?" They were so engrossed with their conversation that they did not notice Mamie coming into the room.

"You can't do a damn thing about it. You baby already sold and the family is coming tomorrow to pick her up. Her name gonna be Gina."

"Who is getting my baby," Savannah asked, mad and scared at the same time.

"Don't you worry about that. That is for me to know and me to know only. Miss Gemini, take her back to her room so she can get some rest. You need to rest yourself, you due any day now yourself."

"Miss Mamie, can't my momma and daddy come get the baby? That's what I want, for my momma and daddy to come get me and her."

"You are only twelve years old so let me explain the rules to you. You got pregnant with no husband; that means your baby can't come home with you. And your momma and daddy don't want no bastard child living with them. So just give me the baby and get the hell out of here. Gemini, take her to her room."

Mamie reached down and took the sleeping baby out of Savannah's arms to place her back in the crib. Gemini grabbed her arm. "You are going to let her hold her baby as long as she needs to or I'm gonna kick your black sorry ass. She ain't never gonna see her baby again and she needs to hold her baby and talk with her to say the things she will never be able to say to her years from now. So you are going to let her spend time with her baby or I swear to God you will be spending time in the hospital and in jail when I get through telling the police what you are doing here. And don't think that I won't 'cause I will. I ain't got nothing to lose right now and everybody knows I'm crazy." Mamie knew to back down. She would bide her time until that crazy bitch had her baby, then she would have her revenge. Besides, she had a good little racket going on here and she did not want the police to come around snooping. The local police didn't give a damn about black children; there was money to be made. But if their arrangement got out, they would be on it like flies on shit.

Mamie left the room and let Savannah and Gemini spend time with the baby. Two hours later, she returned and asked if Savannah had had enough time and was told no. Two hours after that when she returned, Savannah handed over her child to Mamie and she and Gemini returned to the birthing room. She cried all evening long.

Gemini felt so helpless and decided that she would find out who the family was that was coming to take Savannah's baby from her. But until then, she had to get some sleep. Later, as she lay in her bed, Gemini prayed for the first time in a long time that someday Savannah and her daughter would be reunited and be the family that Savannah wanted. She fell asleep at the thought that her prayer would be answered.

Savannah stayed in the room overnight and the next day was placed back into her room by Cora. She looked so pitiful to Gemini and she could do nothing to cheer her up. Mamie came by to say that the family was coming later on in the day to take the baby and wanted Savannah to know that her child was going to a good home. That did little to comfort Savannah and when Mamie left she burst into tears. Gemini tried to comfort her.

"Don't worry, Savannah, I will find out who is getting your baby and I will let you know."

"But how, Gemini, how can you find out when all this is done secretly? Remember last month when Ruthann Summers had her baby, all that was done without her knowing. She will never see her boy again; and she had to go back home to her stepfather and you know what he did to her."

"Don't you worry, I'm gonna find out for you, I promise; just like I did for Ruthann."

Later that morning Gemini snuck to the drawing room where the family that was taking Savannah's baby sat, and hid. A man and woman, very well dressed sat on the couch with Mamie's attorney, the man who arranged the adoptions. They all stood up when Mamie entered carrying little Gina and placed her in the woman's arms. Gemini noticed that there did not seem to be any emotion being displayed by the man, although the woman smiled at the baby and looked at her husband. Gemini was able to hear the conversation between the couple, the attorney, and Mamie. She also saw money being exchanged; it did look like a lot. Then the couple left. After Mamie and the attorney left the room, Gemini followed and went back into the room she shared with Savannah.

"It's all done. Little Gina is gone with her new family. They seem like a nice couple, Dr. and Mrs. David Ban."

At the sound of the names, Savannah sat straight up in bed. "What did you say they names were?"

"Dr. David and Mrs. Ban. I think Bitch Wells called her Nato, or something like that."

"It's Minetta, her name is Minetta." Savannah burst into tears.

"How you know what her name is?"

Savannah was sobbing uncontrollably when she replied, "She's the mother of the man who raped me. Oh, Gemini, my rapist's parents are going to raise my baby!"

I stayed with Savannah for about an hour, trying to convince her to fight for her life, but she would not hear of it. She told me the story of the events that led up to David Ban joining his ancestors, but I did not flinch a bit, even when she told me about the events that led to Gina's death. I wanted to cry with her, not just for her but for me and my baby, the baby I never saw and wondered about daily. I wanted to grab her parents up and kick them dead in their asses for what they failed to do as parents. I wanted to call my parents and tell them how much I hurt knowing that I could never see my child, even though I was raped and the baby was better off.

I was glad David Ban was dead. I hoped that he was in the deepest part of hell next to the serial killers, child murderers, and rapists. He was a child predator himself in the worst way, and no one ever did anything to stop him. He had destroyed the lives of a lot of young girls and it did not stop after he left Kingsford Heights, it got worse.

Chapter 7

David Ban

Kingsford Heights is located in the county of Laporte, Indiana about two hours east of Chicago. Laporte is part of what is called the Michiana area. The county name, which was founded in 1832, is French for "the door," which the French so named after discovering a natural opening in the dense forest that used to exist in the region, providing a gateway to lands farther west.

Kingsford Heights has a low population of blacks, roughly nine percent, unlike Gary, which in 1986 had a population of ninety-eight percent black. Most of the blacks in Kingsford Heights work in South Bend or Michigan City. The town has one black doctor, Dr. David Ban Sr., three black churches, and one black funeral director.

David Allen Ban Jr. looked into the mirror and imagined his father and mother standing in front of him as he pulled the trigger on the imaginary gun he held in his hands. Pow, one to the head for his mother; pow, pow, two to the head for his father; and pow, pow, pow, three for the little shit his momma held in her hands, his supposed child.

He didn't understand why his parents insisted on raising that baby. So damn what his father was orphaned and did not want his grandchild to grow up as he did. What the hell made them think the baby was his? After all, it wasn't his fault "little miss prissy" got pregnant. He pulled out in time, so what was the problem. They act like it was his fault, she was the one that came on to him. They all did, the little shits, always looking at him and asking for it with their looks. Then after he plucked their "cherries," they always pretended like they didn't like it, but he knew better. All females, old and young, liked it when he plucked their cherries. Old Miss Rachel, his eighth grade teacher that nobody liked, loved it when he used to have sex with her. She was the one that started him on his road to sexual greatness. He was thirteen and she was thirty-five, she was old. He remembered the first time Miss Rachel approached him, it was after class and he had been held for detention for talking. He really didn't know what was happening until she started to undress him and his erection was so noticeable that she laughed. He could not control himself and when she forced him into her, he felt repulsed and excited at the same time. She was as black as his mama was and he hated the site of her, but both hated and loved what she made him do. Their messing around went on for a long time until his father caught them and threatened to have Miss Rachel run out of town. Then the old bastard started with Miss Rachel himself. The old bastard had to have everything David had. When he was fifteen, he started in on young girls because they were easy to get and they were too scared to tell. He would be in control, not like when he was with Miss Rachel. Monica Richards was the first of his conquests. She was twelve going on nineteen, with a butt as big as Texas. She was light skinned, big boned, and had long, pretty hair. All his women had to have long hair; good hair, not the nappy nigga stuff. Monica didn't say a word, she just whimpered until he was done, then put on her panties and ran home, but not before he put the fear of David Ban in her. He told her that he would kill her and her cat if she told anyone. She never did.

Next came Lisa Campbell, the pretty, light-skinned daughter of the only black undertaker in Kingsford Heights. His daddy and Mr. Campbell did business together, his daddy always got a kick back for everybody he had sent to the funeral home. Mr. Campbell's wife was dark skinned and everyone knew that when Lisa was born she wasn't none of Mr. Campbell's child. But he raised her as his own, which suited David just fine because she was a real prize. She never told their little secret either. But he did notice one day that she was gone, folks say she went up north to live with her aunt and go to school up there. Rumor had it that she was pregnant even thought she was only eleven. Wasn't his fault though; after all, he had pulled out early just as he did with little miss prissy, Savannah.

He was quite skilled at what he did best. He was twenty years old by the time he raped Savannah. If there were such a thing as love at first sight, well then she had it when she first saw him. He could tell, he could always tell. Females just seemed to look at him with his light skin, his light brown hair, and yes, he had light blue eyes. How many black men had light blue eyes just like that Cool Hand Luke dude? Yeah, he looked like a white man and that was what females liked about him; that was why he could get any female he wanted.

He was sitting outside of his father's office when little Miss Savannah Gill and her father, Rev. Earl Gill, stepped outside after a visit with the doctor. Savannah was cute in her little pink dress with white polka dots, she always wore dresses. Rev. Gill was too good to speak to people who did not go to his church so it did not surprise David when they walked *by him and the good reverend did not speak. David did, however, not because his stupid mother tried to teach him to, but just to see if Savannah would speak back.*

"Ah, good morning, Rev. Gill and little Savannah. Y'all ready for the holidays? What is Santa Claus bringing you for Christmas, Miss Savannah?" He knew he had just hit a nerve with the good reverend and waited to hear what he had to say.

"Christmas is for celebrating the birth of the Lord Jesus, not for heathens like you to make a mockery of it with your Santa Claus and all the other lies you sinners tell. Come, Savannah, we do not talk with heathens who haven't the ears to hear the word or the eyes to see the Lord."

Savannah did not utter a word after what her father said, rather she dropped her head and kind of looked at David with her eyes turned up and smiled. That is when he saw the look of love in her eyes and knew she would be his next prize.

"I didn't mean no harm, Rev. David," he replied, trying very hard to sound sincere. The fact is, he could care less what the fat fuck thought, he just wanted to catch the eye of lil' Miss Gill and he had gotten what he wanted. That look, the look that said, "I think that you are the finest man I have ever seen," the eyes said it all.

He got a chance to make his move three days later when he and his mother ran into first lady Leona Gill and Savannah at the local vegetable market. David came with his mother every Saturday to get collard, turnip, mustard, and kale greens to cook for Sunday dinner. David hated his mother from the time he realized she was blacker than black. He always wondered why his father, who was half-white and could have had any woman he wanted, would end up with someone so black as his mother. Even his younger sister, Gladys, was light skinned with long hair. But his mother always wore her hair short and she couldn't do anything about that black skin. He came to the conclusion that his father was forced to marry the black bitch because she was pregnant with him. The truth of the matter was that his father married his mother because her father had money and only one daughter at the marrying age. Dr. David Ban had no money and no wife, so the situation evened itself out. Sam Williams got a son-in-law, and Dr. David Ban got a wife and the money to open his own practice.

Savannah looked cute in her yellow dress trimmed in green lace. Her mother didn't look so bad. Minetta Gill, even though she was a minister's wife, had a body to die for. She looked good too, in her green dress, and he wondered if he could get next to her too; make it a threesome, mother, daughter, and him.

He perched himself alongside the tomatoes waiting for them to come by. When they approached him he put on his best look of innocence and spoke to them.

"Well what a fine morning, ladies. How are both of you doing today? God is good." He looked straight into the eyes of Mrs. Gill and saw the look of acceptance in her face.

"Well good morning, David Jr. You are right, God is good. What brings you here this morning?"

"Mama is over there getting greens for Sunday dinner and I insisted on coming here and picking her some tomatoes," he lied. "She loves them with greens for Sunday dinner."

"I do too, David Jr., and Elder Gill loves them too. That is why I stopped here, to get a couple to go with the greens that he likes so much. Say hello to David Jr., Savannah. Where are your manners?

David turned and looked at Savannah. Yeah, she liked him all right. He saw the look that most girls gave him, that "I want you" look.

"Hi, David," Savannah said. Unknown to David she was very shy around boys, as were most girls her age.

"And hello to you, Miss Gill. You are looking mighty cute today. I know the young men will be standing in line to see you when you grow up. I don't know what Elder Gill is gonna do." And he didn't give a damn either, she would be spoiled goods by then, he would see to that.

"Elder Gill don't even wanna think about that right now," Mrs. Gill replied, "he just wants her to go to college and be somebody. Look at all those black people on TV now; he wants her to do something like that. You would think that he wanted her to get married and have a bunch of babies, but no, her father wants her to be someone great and make a strong mark on the world."

"Well I can see that she is well on her way," David Jr. said. "She has that look." Savannah's cheeks turned ruby red at the sound of David's remarks. Boy, he was so cute, with his light skin. And did he really have blue eyes? Yes, he sure did. He even had light brown hair. All the girls at school talked about him and how he looked like that white actor everybody thought was so cute. She did not see it at first, but now she could see it plain as day.

"Well, you ladies have a good day and remember me in your prayers," David said as he walked away, knowing that he would see Savannah again.

"We will, David Jr. And tell your mama I said hello and we must get together next week and plan the next PTA meeting at the school."

"Yeah right, bitch. I'll tell her the day after hell freezes over," David said to himself. "Oh, I will, Mrs. Gill, and I'll be seeing you real soon, Miss Savannah," David said.

"Yeah, baby girl, big daddy will be seeing you real soon," he thought to himself.

Real soon came two days later on Savannah's way to school. David knew her route to school, where to stand, and just as he predicted, Savannah came around the corner with her schoolbooks in her hand. It did not take much to convince her to let him walk with her to school. After all, anything could happen to her; didn't she hear about that girl in Michigan City that was attacked on her way to school. They had never caught the guy.

David convinced Savannah to take the short cut through the woods behind Davis's store; it would get her there quicker. He even held her hand as they walked through the woods and was still holding her hand when he forced her down on the ground, took off her panties, and raped her. Savannah offered little resistance, she was only twelve and David was twenty. When he finished with her, he made her put on her panties and walk to school, vowing to say that she threw herself at him if she told anyone. Savannah kept her mouth shut.

Later that night when she got home, she took her panties off and washed them in the sink. She took the green dress that she was wearing and hid it in the closet. Then she dressed herself for bed, climbed into bed, and cried herself to sleep hoping this would all go away.

It didn't go away; it got worse as time wore on. Savannah noticed her clothes were getting smaller and her stomach bigger. She knew where babies came from and figured that she was pregnant but she could not tell her parents. She decided to keep quiet until she could figure out what to do. Six months later, she was gaining weight in all the wrong places, much to her parent's alarm. They took her to Dr. Ban's office who confirmed what they had already suspected; Savannah was pregnant. That night at the Gill house, all hell broke loose. After a tirade of calling her every name in the book but a child of God, Savannah's father and grandmother finally got Savannah to reveal the name of the father. Horrified, Elder Gill, called the Bans and when the two families met, it was agreed that Savannah would be sent away to have the baby. David denied everything, stating that he did not have anything to do with what happened to Savannah Gill. His father wanted to call the police, but his mother would not hear of it. So, Dr. Ban made another decision, either David enlisted in the Army and get sent to Vietnam, or he went to jail. David enlisted the next day.

I left Savannah and returned to the office, forgetting to take my medicine. I was feeling the beginning signs of the euphoric feeling when I am going into a manic state. The medicine that I was taking would curve that feeling, I needed to maintain, and be at my best for Savannah. But when I returned to the office, I forgot once again. Most of the staff was out and so I had complete privacy as I sat at my desk to make my notes. I was going to need Antoinette to secure a list of the witnesses from the DA's office and I wanted copies of all the footage from the TV stations that had been there the day of the shooting. I would contact Bookie later; I really needed him to do some investigating for me. There was something bothering me about what Savannah had revealed to me and I needed answers ASAP.

Bookie was in his office and arrived in mine less than a minute after I called him. He was his usual self and when he noticed that I was not responding to his "all my Gemini" jokes, he got serious, sat down, and watched me for a minute until I was ready to speak.

"Bookie, what do you know about David Ban's wife?"

"Nothin' much, except that she's a widow today, why?"

"Savannah told me that she was the guest of Glenda Ban to attend the press conference, but they were not really friends."

"So what's wrong with that?"

"Nothing and that is what is bothering me, why did she invite Savannah to the press conference and not other people more closely connected to Ban?"

"Well how much more close can you get than Savannah, she did have a baby with him."

"When she was eleven years old and the bastard raped her. Is it possible that the Glenda Ban knew about Gina being Savannah and Ban's child?"

"Possible, but what difference would it make, Gina was his personal assistant and he passed her off as his sister. Well, legally she was his sister, according to records. The Bans adopted Gina in 1971 when she was three days old."

"They bought her!"

"Well they may have paid money to get her, but to keep her they had to go through legal channels, which they did. So, it must have been a private adoption."

"So it would not have made a difference to Mrs. Ban whether or not Gina was the daughter or not. Legally, she was his sister."

"But how would she have found out about Gina, do you think Ban would have told her?"

"No, but I still cannot shake the fact that Glenda Ban had an ulterior motive for inviting Savannah to the press conference. I need to find out what it was."

"So you want me to pay a visit to the Ban house?"

"No, Bookie, I will pay a visit to Glenda. I need to do this one myself. What did you find out about the gun?

"It was a forty-five, nice piece according to the police. The gun was registered to Savannah. Oh, I found out the scoop on Gina Ban. She committed suicide last year. Put one bullet in her head one week after receiving her master's. She was also engaged; seems she was going to marry Ronny Washington."

"The Ronny Washington of the Chicago Bears?"

"One and the same. It seems that Ban was opposed to the marriage and threatened to ruin Gina and Washington if they married."

"That is strange. What did he have against Washington?"

"I don't know, all my Gemini, but I get paid to find out things like that."

"And on your way out, tell Antoinette I need to see her."

"All my Gemini, are you okay, how are you holding up?"

"I've been better, I've been worse."

"Hang in there, baby." And Bookie was off. I was not alone for long; Antoinette came in after Bookie and sat down.

"What's happening, boss lady? What cha need?"

"I need to contact Glenda Ban and pay my respects. Get her on the phone for me. I need to speak with her."

"Do you think that will go over well, the woman defending her husband's killer paying her respects?"

"Why not, Glenda and I have sat on several committees to gather. It is expected."

Antoinette left my office and placed the call. Glenda was not shocked to hear from me, she was expecting my call. She had heard that I was representing Savannah and said it would be okay if I dropped by. "Two o' clock today would be fine," she had said. Then we said our good-byes. This was not going to be easy.

I left the office at one p.m. in order to get to the Ban's house on time. The traffic was bad this time of day but I did manage to make it on time. The Ban house sits on a hill near the lake in our city. The houses there are owned by some of the riches blacks in the city. Quinn has a house there.

The Ban house was a two-story brick home with a big bay window in the front and a bay window over the garage. The driveway wound around the house and the lawns seem as if they stretched for miles. I parked my car next to a black Cadillac and walked to the front door. After ringing the doorbell, I was greeted by a very pleasant woman who turned out to be Glenda Ban's mother, Sonja Dunlap, a very prestige's person in her own right. Mrs. Dunlap led me to the sitting room where Glenda and her brother, Terrence, and sister-in-law, Sabrina Dunlap, were. Terrence was a top-notch attorney and Sabrina was a high school principal. All eyes looked at me suspiciously.

Glenda walked over to me as I entered the room. Unlike Ban she was dark skinned but with the complexion to die for. Her eyes were almond shaped and her hair hung to her shoulders. It was thick and showed signs of age by the amount of gray it had in it. Her hands were small, as were her feet. She was maybe six foot one in her stocking feet and as thin as ever. At one time Glenda was a Paris runway model and had later settled for being Mrs. David Ban. Now she was the widow Ban.

"Gemini, I have been expecting you. You know my brother and sister-in-law, don't you?" We all exchanged niceties before I sat down. I had a feeling that Terrence was there for more than just support.

"Thank you for allowing me to visit you in your time of grief."

"I understand you are defending Savannah Wooten," Terrence asked just as I was sitting down in what felt like pure heaven.

"Yes, I am, we served on several charity committees together and the firm felt that I could best serve her." I eyed him with suspicion. Did he know about Savannah and me? "Which is one of the reasons I am here, but first let me offer my condolences on your loss."

"Thank you, Gemini," Glenda responded. "Now what is the other basis for you visit."

"I just wanted to ask a few questions. First, how close are you and my client?"

"Not very. Like you, we serve on several committees together and she and David's sister were friends."

I noticed that she said "David's sister" and not "my sister-in-law," which I thought was strange but put it in the back of my mind.

"Were she and Gina friends?" I hoped that I sounded convincing.

"Well, I don't know how close they were, I just know that she was very upset about the suicide last year."

"Is that why you invited Savannah to the press conference?"

I saw Glenda glance at her brother before she attempted to answer the question, but before she could, Terrence answered.

"My sister wanted as many friends as possible to be on hand for the press conference to support her husband as well as very influential people. Savannah is a well-established businesswoman in the community so quite naturally my sister had the foresight to invite her. Only now does she realize it was a mistake." Very nice response, I thought. He was very good at what he did.

"And you say that Savannah seemed upset when your sister-in-law committed suicide last year. Was she upset at your husband also?"

Terrence answered for his sister. "Well, yes, as a matter of fact she was. She was good friends with Ronny Washington and she wanted the two of them to get married, but David would not hear of it and Savannah was upset."

"What did David have against Ronny Washington?" I asked, but somewhere in the back of my mind a voice, a very tiny voice, was yelling, "You have an idea why; don't you, Gemini?"

"He just wanted better for Gina, that's all" Terrence seemed to be doing all of the talking. Glenda said nothing, which told me a lot."

"If you don't mind me saying, Ronny Washington has a multi-million dol-lar contract with the Bears, with drop-dead good looks, and he graduated from Grambling with honors. How much better can you get?"

"He wanted better for his sister, Ms. Jones. That is all that I can tell you," Terrence Dunlap replied. I could hear the tension in his voice, he did not like the observation that I had made.

"Was Gina an unstable person?" This question got a jolt from Glenda who dropped the drink that she had in her hand.

"I am so sorry; it just upsets me to talk about David's sister like that." Again, there was no mention of Gina's name from Glenda. "Will you excuse me?" Then, very awkwardly, she got up and left the room, Terrence's wife Sabrina went with her. That just left Terrence, their mother, and me in the room. I wondered why the mother did not get up to see about her daughter.

"Well, as you can see my sister is very upset over this whole affair. You realize that it is very difficult for you to be here as you are representing the woman who allegedly killed my brother-in-law."

"I am glad that you said 'allegedly'."

"You mean you think that she is innocent? Half of the city saw her do it."

"But none of the cameras actually have her pulling the trigger." This brought a look of surprise on the face of Terrence Dunlap, attorney at law.

"But she was standing there with the gun," he replied. Was he trying to con-vince me that my client did it?

"Actually the gun was at her feet. The TV audience did not see her pull the trigger." That got me another look of surprise from my colleague.

"Well, you may have a case of reasonable doubt on your hands," he said, but I noticed a quick look of disgust on his face. What was that all about?

"Looks like it, which only means that the real killer is still out there."

"Or your client dropped the gun after she shot my brother-in-law. If you will excuse me, I will go and see about my sister."

He got up and left the room. That left just their mother and me in the room together.

"I will be leaving now," I told her and got up so that she could escort me to the door. She did not move.

"I do not want you upsetting my daughter again, Ms. Jones. She is very upset by this whole affair. She and David were going to go on a second honeymoon, right after the press conference. Now she will be burying him, instead. I am try-ing to convince her to go on the trip after the funeral; it will give her a chance to get herself together; first David's sister and now David. It is too much for one person to have to bear." What was the deal about not calling Gina by her name?

"Well, I hope I do not have to trouble her again." By this time she had gotten up and was escorting me to the door.

"I hope so as well, Ms. Jones." I did not like the tone in her voice but I ignored it.

"You take care, Mrs. Dunlap. Have a nice day and, again, I am sorry for your loss."

She never replied, but simply closed the door behind me.

In my car driving back to the office, I called Bookie who answered the phone on the first ring. "Where are you, Gemini?"

"On my way back to the office, now I need for you to do something for me. First, David and his wife were supposed to go on a second honeymoon after the press conference, find out where. If they were getting a divorce, why would they be going on a second honeymoon? Also, get in touch with Ronny Washington, see if you can get him to meet with me and discuss Gina's suicide. I am on my way back to the office but I need to see Savannah again."

"Well, you better hurry; I was going to call you. Savannah's been trans-ported back to the hospital. It doesn't look good."

I did a U-turn in the middle of the street.

Chapter 8

Methodist Hospital was just a few miles from where I was, so I arrived within minutes of the call with Bookie. The press was waiting outside and as I approached, I was recognized and the sharks started circling. I walked past the group of reporters all the time stating that I would be holding a press conference soon and walked into the hospital. Savannah had been admitted to the oncology floor and as I approached the room, I saw not one but two police personnel guarding the door. Why did one woman need so much security? As I entered the room, Savannah was lying in bed having a conversation with her doctor. Dr. Helen Cahill had a reputation of being the best in the field and I was glad she was on the case.

Savannah seemed to brighten up as I entered. "Hey, Gemini. Girl, I told Antoinette not to bother you with this; I am right as rain."

"Yeah, that's what Noah said after he built the ark and look what happened." I knew that was a stupid remark, but I was mad at her and I did not care who knew it.

I introduced myself to the doctor, who was very pleasant but I could tell by the look on her face, things were not good.

Dr. Cahill and I were just discussing why I will not be making an appearance at my trial. Tell her what you told me, Dr. Cahill." The doctor turned to me and repeated what she had just told her patient.

"Savannah is in stage four of breast cancer. The cancer has spread every-where, and it is only a matter of time. At this point even if I could get her to change her mind and start chemotherapy, it would not do her any good. The cancer is too far gone."

"Tell her how long, Dr. Cahill. I need for her to get herself ready."

"Savannah, shut the hell up!" I shouted at her, all the anger and frustration coming out like water when a damn bursts! "I wouldn't have to be preparing myself if you had for once thought of someone else other than yourself. What about the people you are leaving behind; and if you think that I am going to stop representing you then you are out of your mind."

"Ms. Jones, I know how upset you are about this but this is not the time to explode. This is the time, however, to help Savannah come up with a course of action. She has three to six months at the most."

"The DA is not going to allow anything but a stay in the prison hospital until she dies, although I can try to get her to stay here. She can pay for her own hospital stay so it won't be a burden on the taxpayers."

"I just want to go in peace. I want to be with Gina."

"May I have a word with my client, Dr. Cahill?" Dr. Cahill nodded, and left the room. I turned on Savannah with all the fury I had in me.

"You know damn well you did not kill David Ban. Who did it, Savannah? Who are you covering for?"

"What makes you think I am covering for someone, Gemini? I killed David Ban and that is that. Now leave me the hell alone about this mess."

"This mess? This mess! You say you shot a man on TV and all you can say is that this is a mess?" And now I have a hunch that you are covering for someone else. Why is that? Why do I have that feeling, Savannah?"

"Cause you crazy as hell; that's why, Gemini. You are crazy as hell. I told you I did it and how, and you know why. Now what the hell else do you want from me?"

"The truth, Savannah, I want the truth. I went to see Glenda Ban today and her brother did all the talking. He is one of the best defense lawyers in the city. Quinn tried to recruit him, but he went to Turner, Dean, and Weismann instead, and will probably make partner soon. Now, him doing all the talking tells me a lot. Also, David was against Gina marrying Ronny Washington. Why would he be against her marrying the best running back in football who currently has a fifteen million dollar contract with the Bears? And then there is the fact that no one in that household calls Gina by her first name, that is also cause for me to listen to that little voice in my ear telling me that you and that family have not been completely honest with me."

"You ain't so crazy after all, girlfriend, but I am tired right now. I need my rest." She looked exhausted by our conversation. I felt so sorry for her, but I was mad at her at the same time. I knew she was hiding something, I just did not know what. But I was going to find out.

I left the hospital and headed straight to the office. Antoinette was waiting for me when I walked in. She told me that Quinn had stopped by to see me but he had left for the day. That meant to stop by his office first thing in the morning.

I did a little more paper work, and then decided to call it quits. I told Antoinette she could leave early if she wanted; I was leaving for the day. That was all she needed to hear, she beat me out the door.

My drive home gave me time to think and time to reflect on my past, and Savannah's and David's for that matter. David had caused a lot of suffering throughout the years, and no one seemed to learn about it. How did a man as corrupt and sick as David Ban get to where he was before three bullets sent him to his ancestors? How did he manage to keep Gina a secret from the rest of the world? These were answers that I needed to know if I was going to get my client off for murder. "David Ban, you son of a bitch," I thought. "How the hell did you get us into this?"

Saigon, South Vietnam, 1971

David was pissed as he and a handful of soldiers landed in Saigon for his first and only tour. Why in the hell did he have to end up here? Damn his father and damn that bitch Savannah. How in the hell was he supposed to live at home when the reminder of his being seduced was currently shitting and pissing in his home while he was stuck out here in the middle of hell? Well, he was going to make sure that he got out of this place alive. He wasn't going to die over here for some damn fool principle of glory and honor. Glory and honor his ass.

It was hot as a whore on a Saturday night out here in Viet damn Nam, and if he did not watch it, he was going to get even darker than he did when he was in basic training.

The Army was a pain in the ass, but it was better than going to jail for rape. He did not rape that girl; she wanted what he gave her, and boy did he give it to her good. Now her damn baby was living with his parents and his black ass mama was really drooling over her. Gina, that was what his mother named her after her black ass grandmother. He hated dark-skinned women; he hated their nasty skin, their smell, everything about them. Miss Rachel and his mama were at the top of the list.

White girls were okay, he had screwed a few while he was stationed at Fort Campbell in Kentucky. Why did they send him to a big city some place where he could practice his moves on the young girls? He liked them young; they never complained and they worshipped him, the black Cool Hand Luke.

At Fort Campbell, he had gotten into it with most of the brothas in his platoon. Especially the brothas from the East Coast, they were always talking about him being an uncle tom, just because he hung out with the whites in his platoon. Those crazy East Coast niggas were always talking about black power this and black power that. But they always put him down 'cause he wasn't into that black shit. They were just jealous of him, with his white man looks.

He hated his sergeant too. He was always picking on him calling him a 'yella nigga.' If he had gotten a chance to kick that Sambo's ass, he would have. Sergeant Marvin Stewart was black as his mama and just as ugly. They could have been brother and sister.

Now he was over here, with the rest of the group and he was going to try to make the best of it until his tour was up.

Vietnam was at the height of the war in 1971. He hated the heat, the smell, and the people. He hated everything about being over there except when he could go to Bangkok for a little R & R. He would hang out at the Soul Sistas' Bar where most of the blacks hung out. There he could have all the young girls that he wanted, but he was only doing them a favor, they all wanted him too.

He never messed with the Vietnamese women, the Army discouraged it, although a few of his friends did not heed the Army's warnings and got involved with them. It wasn't because they were not appealing; most of them were small as children. It was because of the "black syph" that he did not want to mess with them.

It was rumored that soldiers who contacted "the black syph," which was a deadly form of syphilis, were never allowed to go home. Catching that shit meant certain death. When one of his friends contracted the disease, it was rumored that he was reported missing in action to his family back in Iowa and died in one of the army hospitals. Nor was his body shipped home for burial, he just simply disappeared. That is what happened to all the soldiers who contacted "the black syph," they could never return home.

And that is why he waited to go to Bangkok to have his fun. There they made sure that the girls were clean for the enjoyment of those who desired them. The Army didn't encourage the soldiers to have sex with the women, but the word was that if you could not resist, make sure the girl you were with had her health card; not that it made any difference, a lot of those cards were fake.

Bangkok and little girls made his time in the Army tolerable. Who was it that sang that song, "Thank Heaven for Little Girls?"

He arrived home in the fall of 1974, crazy and hungry for the girls he left behind. His parents did not allow him to return home, so he moved to Michigan City and started going to school. His good looks did not get him far, so he had to rely on his brain, which really wasn't so bad. When he finished his degree in political science, he found a teaching job in one of the local junior high schools. David was in heaven.

By the time David started teaching school, it was 1978. He had not had any contact with his parents in all that time. So when he received a message from the coroner's office in Kings Ford Heights, he knew it was about them. The coroner informed him that his parents had been killed in a car accident and that he was listed as the next of kin. It was just the two of them in the car and he needed to come to the office to make an official identification.

David made the trip from Michigan City to Kingsford Heights in ten minutes. He identified both of his parents and was told by the policeman handling the case that his sister Gina was with child welfare and that they would like to speak with him.

David met with child welfare authorities, who informed him that Gina was in foster care and that a lovely couple would probably want to adopt her. All David could think about was the money from his parents that Gina would get. The poor little orphan would appeal to any jury after he decided to sue the people who killed his parents. He decided that he needed the money and demanded to see his "sister." As her only living relative, he would be taking her home with him and raise her himself, spending the money he would get from the insurance company as well as the life insurance his father had. He was sure that Gina was the sole beneficiary and as her next of kin, he would have to have access to the money in order to raise her. He could live like a king.

So, two days after his parents did him a favor and died and seven years after the birth of his "sister," David saw Gina for the first time in seven years. It was love at first sight. The minute he laid eyes on her he knew she would be his. He would never let her go. Wasn't love grand!

When seven-year-old Gina walked into the room and saw the brother she did not remember, a cold chill swept through her. There was something not quite right about the way he looked at her. But at her age, she could not tell what it was. But he was her brother, she had seen pictures of him at her parent's house, but they never talked about him.

David knelt down to talk with his daughter and told her about their parent's death. He held her in his arms as she cried and he assured her that he would take care of her and that they would be a family. The money would assure them that their life would be good!

The funeral for his parents took place three days later. The church was packed; half of the city came to pay their respects, including the mayor and two city councilmen. His father had planned every detailed of their burial and had paid in advance for the services. Good David thought, as he, Gina, and most of the town of Kingsford Heights stood at the graveside of one of the most influential black couples in town, that there would be more money for him to spend. And, of course, he had to make sure that his precious Gina had everything a girl with her beauty should have. He would give her the world and she would be his forever. Of course, he would have to take a wife, someone who would be a good mother to Gina, but he would never love anyone as much as he loved her.

A week after the funerals, David met with his parents' attorney who informed him that his father had provided well for Gina and that as her guardian he would have access to her trust fund but he would have to account for every penny. Any monies from the lawsuit would be split between the two of them. The practice had to be sold and half the money placed into Gina's trust fund which would be hers on her twenty-first birthday. Of course, he and Gina could continue to live in the family home if he wanted, but David wanted no part of that hell house, too many bad memories of his black ass momma and self-righteous daddy. So, the house would be sold along with the practice and the money would be equally divided between David and Gina.

David figured he was looking at a cool million between the lawsuit and the selling of the practice and the house. Gina's trust fund was a little over a million and she would be getting the Social Security benefits from both parents, black momma had been a teacher for twelve years before she married his father.

As David left the lawyer's office, he felt as if God were smiling on him. His parents were dead, he would soon be rich, and he had the love of his life, his little Gina. Man, life was good!

Chapter 9

What was I thinking when I took this case? This was bringing back too many memories about my baby, Gina, Bitch Wells, and the things that were done to me after I had my child—hell, the things that were done to me while I was in labor. If I had half a mind I would get on the freeway, drive to Marion, find that bitch Mamie, and kick her ass I still hate her to this day Why I don't hate my parents I do not know They were only doing what they thought was best for me, but it wasn't as if I was a wreck when that boy raped me I spent two years of my life getting myself together and wondering where my baby was I wondered if he was doing okay and who had bought and raised him as their own. I wondered why I hadn't tried to find him and tell him how much I wanted to keep him but couldn't because I was young and mentally ill I wanted to tell him that I wished things were different that I could have raised him myself but I was young and sick I would explain to him that my parents were not going to add to their burdens by raising another child who might have the same problems that I had My mind was racing as I drove home that night So much for skipping my medication.

Dr. Gray's answering service received my call and informed me that she was gone for the day and asked if they wanted me to get in touch with her. I told the nice, preppy voice on the other end that I had Elmonda's number and would call her myself at home. I also told her that she sounded so nice and professional on the phone and that it made people feel good to know someone like her was on the other end of the phone when they called in a crisis. I asked her if she considered getting into the health field, that she would be an asset to any hospital or doctor's office, and then made myself get off the phone and quickly called Elmonda.

She answered on the first ring. "Gemini, are you okay?"

"How did you know it was me, I never said a word. Did you know by the way I breathed into the phone or what? Now I know; you willed me to call you. ESP, the best invention since sliced bread."

"You gave me your word you would start taking your medication. I need to see you right away have Bookie bring you in tomorrow. Do I need to come over, Gemini?"

"I will." I hung up and the phone rang, it was Bookie. He was somewhere in a bar getting his drink on.

"I am on my way, all my Gemini; you have been a bad girl. I will let myself in with the key you have under the door."

"Bookie, thanks."

"You're welcome, beautiful; be there in twenty minutes."

Bookie really was my friend.

"It takes a few doses of the medication in a person's system before they return to normal. My manic episode was not a severe one, but I needed to be at my best for Savannah's sake.

Bookie arrived about half an hour later. He found my medication and made sure that I took it. I was pacing the floor by then, although I had been instructed to remain on the couch by Bookie. When a person goes into a manic state, it is hard to keep still. I knew the stress of this case was affecting me, but I had to see this through. I had to get Savannah off, if I could only stay sane.

Bookie handed my medication to me and a large glass of water, which I completely drank before handing him the glass. My thoughts were racing so fast and my desire to talk was overwhelming. So I did just that, I talked.

"Ever since we were put in that Bitch Wells's home and became roommates, I have always felt compelled to help Savannah. It was tough being in that home. I was fifteen; she was twelve. I hated Bitch Wells and she was afraid of me, that's why I was able to protect Savannah. Wells hated her on site. Why she gave her to me was beyond my scope of thinking but she did, she gave Savannah to me to protect and that is what I did. I held her in my arms when she found out that David Ban's parents adopted her baby. How could anyone in their right mind let the parents of the rapist raise that child? But I guess back then all Bitch Wells cared about was the money. And the David Bans cared about not having one of their own grow up in a stranger's household. I wanted to keep my baby, too. I was raped by a guy I went to school with but my parents said no and so I had to give up my baby to Bitch Wells who wouldn't even let me see my son. Yes, Bookie, I have a son somewhere in this world. I wonder if he is trying to get in touch with me. I wonder what kind of man he has become. I wonder if he will hate me if he ever finds me…"

I worked from home for the next few days just until I started to feel like myself again. Bookie came by every day with information from Antoinette that I needed to prepare for Savannah's defense. Quinn called every day to consult with me, and my team came by for meetings with me once a day while I was out.

It was tough for me. Stress is not good for people who are bipolar, but I had great support and I was determine to help my client.

I had Bookie check in on Savannah on a daily basis. She was still in the hospital and was sticking to her guns not to have treatment. She wanted to die.

I still managed to make the arraignment and was able to persuade the judge to let my client stay in the hospital for treatment, at her expense. The ADA made the motion that she be examined by their doctors to determine if she would be fit to stand trial.

In the meantime, the press was running with everything that they could get their hands on about the case. People were outraged that their beloved David Ban had been gunned down and they wanted justice. The TV news stations also had to admit that not one of them had coverage of Savannah actually killing Ban on the air, just footage of the police arresting Savannah after finding the gun at her feet.

That would help with Savannah's defense and the things that Bookie was finding out about Ban made my skin crawl. How in the world did such an insane and evil man become the pillar of the community, a man that everyone, black, white, brown, crippled, and crazy adored? I was going to discuss with Quinn about putting David Ban on trial, but I wanted to discuss it with Savannah first.

I returned to work a week later. The medicine was working and Bookie was checking with me every day to make sure I was taking it.

I talked with Savannah every day, trying to convince her to fight, but she would only shake her head and turn away from me.

This made me angry, but it did not matter. I was going to fight until the end for her; for us and the hell we went through at the hands of Bitch Wells.

Hell on Earth, Home of Mamie Wells

It was time for Savannah to leave. The parents of David Ban had come two days earlier and taken her baby home with them. Now her parents and Nana were coming to take her home. Back to her little pink room with the stuffed toys on the other twin bed. Back to the God-fearing parents and self-righteous grandmother who had deserted her when she really needed them; all in the name of God, and appearances.

Gemini watched Savannah as she packed her suitcase and she knew the pain her friend was in. Not just the physical pain but also the emotional pain, which was ten times as worse. Having to leave here without the baby she gave birth to and knowing that the parents of the rapist were going to raise her child, which meant that the rapist was going to be a part of the baby's life, was a torment no one should have to endure. That was a lot for a twelve-year-old to bear. Gemini felt so guilty for her role in Savannah's pain. After all, she was the one who had told Savannah where the baby was going. And although she did not hold Gemini at fault, it did nothing to erase the guilt she felt. Savannah would be scarred for life, and she was partly responsible.

"Gemini," it was Savannah talking to her, "I just want to thank you for all your help. You were here for me and I will never forget you. Are you going to be all right?"

"I'll be fine," Gemini lied, "and Bitch Wells is not going to get the best of me." I think I'm going to put my foot up her ass today, but I won't do it until after you leave."

"Oh, Gemini," Savannah was laughing now, "I ain't never known anyone like you. You cuss like a sailor, you can be happy one minute and angry the next. You are my angel, my cussing angel." She burst into tears with that statement, "You are the only person I know who was in my corner while I was suffering here."

"Damn you, Savannah Gill," Gemini was crying, "will you stop all that crying and shit. I hate it when you do that, and don't be crying when you get home either. Just keep on pushing and enjoy your life and one day maybe you and your daughter will meet and get to know each other. After all, you both live in the same town and it ain't like you live in Chicago. Hell, my ass is larger than Kingsford Heights." She knew that would make Savannah laugh. She was right.

"Gemini, you say the craziest things and you cuss like a sailor, my daddy would have a heart attack if he heard you."

"Then maybe when they come to take you home, I will give him an ear full. Will that make you happy?"

"I don't know; daddy may have something to say on the way home; he tends to go on and on about evilness and stuff like that. Then Nana puts her two cents in, and Lord help us all when that happens. She'll be preaching all the way back to Kings Fort Heights."

The knock at the door startled both of them. In walked Mamie, and the look on her face told them that Savannah's parents had arrived.

"Your parents and grandmother are here to take you home." She was out the door before either of them could respond.

"I'll walk you out, Savannah; I want to see what Chrystians look like."

"You mean 'Christians,' don't you, Gemini?"

"Hell no, I mean Chrytstians. Christians would not have sent you to this hell hole."

Savannah wanted to cry, but Gemini's remark made her laugh instead. She would miss her friend, but she would be strong for her and she would do what Gemini told her to do, she would go home live her life, and try to be happy. She would work hard in school, make a lot of money when she got out, and then she would go and get her baby. They would be a family, she would find her a husband to take care of both of them, and they would all be rich and happy forever.

"I don't think Bitch Wells wants you walking with me, Gemini, I'll just go out with her". She did not want Gemini to see her leave, she knew the tears would flow and she did not want Gemini to see her as weak.

"Savannah Gill, you said a cuss word. You said 'bitch.' Right on, my sista, right on. I taught you well!" They both laughed, hugged each other, and then Savannah was gone.

Mamie was waiting for her outside of the room and as they walked to where her parents were waiting to take her home, Mamie began talking to her in a low and slow tone that made her skin crawl.

"You listen to me, missy. Don't you go tellin' your parents about what went on here. You remember that your crazy friend is still here and you wouldn't want anything to happen to her or her baby now would you? Who knows what could happen to her once she goes into labor. She might die in childbirth and the baby may die too. It's up to you, missy; it's up to you."

They entered the room where Savannah's parents and grandmother were waiting. Mamie turned on her role in such a way that would make Ruby Dee stand up and take notice. She played this role for all the parents.

"Here she is, Reverend and Mrs. Gill. She was just saying her good-byes to her friends. I try to make each girl's departure as easy as possible. They have such a hard time coping with having to give their ba..."

"We won't speak about what happened here, Miss Wells, if you don't mind," Bishop Gill interrupted. "We'll be on our way now. My wife, mother, and I will pray for the lost souls who inhabit this place. We know that it is a hard task the Lord has put upon you and we continue to pray for you as well. The Lord has a place in heaven for you, I only hope these girls will fall down on their knees and thank you and God for being there for them in their time of need."

"God bless you, Reverend. I try to do the Lord's will every day that he allows me to breathe," Mamie said. "And every day I get paid for these bastards, I thank God for my retirement," she thought.

Good byes were said and Mamie walked the family to the door. She noticed that no one really addressed Savannah, they just walked out the door and they were gone. "Good riddance to the little whore and those self-righteous assholes!" Mamie said to herself.

As Savannah walked to the car with her suitcase, her father had refused to take it for her, the tears started to flow. Her mother noticed but said nothing. Her father looked at her with such disgust that she quickly wiped her eyes and walked silently to the car. Nana was praying and walking, praying and walking, and Savannah knew the ride home was going to be silent and long.

Just as she was about to put her suitcase in the car, she heard the voice of Gemini coming from one of the rooms upstairs.

"Hey, Reverend Gill; I hope you, your wife, and your whore of a mother all burn in the deepest, hottest part of hell. And you can all kiss my pregnant ass. Stay strong, Savannah; trouble don't last always."

Savannah smiled.

On the way home, Savannah learned the fate that awaited her because of her sins. Her father had been appointed Bishop of the First district of the Church of God Devine, and that meant that the family would be moving to Gary and would not return to Kingsford Heights. The chances of running into the Bans were good since the town was so small, and they did not want any contact with Savannah's bastard child. They had not even bothered to know the sex of the child and Savannah was instructed that she was not to talk about this sin that she had committed. She would have to pray every day for the rest of her life for what she had put her family through and one day, when she was ready to cross over into the Promised Land, God would forgive her of her sin. In the meantime, she would have to spend the rest of her life making amends to God and to her family for what she allowed Satan to do to her. That meant no TV, no playing outside, no activities at school, church every day, and no friends, except Jesus. He would be her only companion until God called her home.

Chapter 10

A few weeks had past and I received a call from the district attorney's office, which I was expecting, wanting to meet with my client and me. He wanted to bargain. That took us all by surprise until we realized that he knew Savannah was sick and we assumed he did not want to put a terminally ill woman on trial.

I had Antoinette confirm the appointment and as I sat at my desk trying to put together some notes for the meeting that was to take place in two days, Bookie came running in unannounced. The look in his eyes told me that he had something good to tell me.

"All my Gemini, baby have I got the news that is going to set you straight and make you want to make love to me ALL NIGHT LONG!"

"You must have won the lottery," I replied. Bookie was king of the comebacks.

"I said make you want to make love to me all night, not marry me and bear my children."

"All right, Bookie. What is it?"

"I think you need to bring in the whole team to hear this one."

I rang Antoinette. "Have everyone join us in here in five minutes."

I turned to Bookie. "Now, will you tell me first, or will I have to hear it with the rest of the team. I think I need to hear it first."

"Look, y'all, I want the whole team to hear this at the same time. Besides, if I tell you with just the two of us in the room. You may not be able to contain yourself, and I want to wait until I get you home for the loving all of you are going to put on me!" Something told me there was a bit of truth in what he was saying.

The team walked in just before I killed the best investigator in the firm.

"This better be good, Bookie Lyman," Israel said as he walked into the room. "I was on my way to lunch with the cutest Gentile redhead I've have ever had the pleasure of meeting and drooling over."

"Yeah, Bookie, we are all up to our necks in work around here trying to get Ms. Wooten's defense in order, so if you got something we could use, let us know now," Suni chimed in behind Israel.

"Sit down, my people, and behold the powers of Bookie Lyman. First of all, Gemini, what I have to tell you is going to turn this case upside down, but first I want to ask you a question. Did the district attorney call you today for a meeting to discuss a plea?"

"How the hell did you know that?" Antoinette said before I could respond.

"Yes, he did," I replied. "I am meeting with him today. I figure he doesn't want to put a sick woman on trial, even if she is accused of murdering one of this city's most loved assholes."

"That sounds like a logical reason to want to plea bargain, but I can give you one better."

"Because the film crew doesn't have footage of her shooting Ban, we know that," Malcolm George said sarcastically. I really don't like that smart-ass.

"That would be a good reason too, but he has witnesses who say that they saw Savannah shoot Ban."

"Whose testimonies I will tear to shreds when I get them on the stand."

"My point exactly," Bookie shot back.

"So, Bookie, what reason would the DA have for wanting to make a deal if he knows about the footage, but has witnesses, and doesn't want a sick and dying woman on trial?" I asked, getting pissed at this point with him.

"Cause he don't have the murder weapon!" Bookie said before sitting back and letting it sink in. "That's right, sports fans, the GUN IS MISSING!"

We all sat in silence for a minute to let it all sink in and as if we were all speaking with one voice, we all responded, "HOW THE HELL DID THAT HAPPEN?"

Michigan City, IN: Where David's Luck Changed

David Ban was on his way to a meeting that was going to change his life and make him the man his dead and rotting father didn't think he could be.

Being a schoolteacher and being so close to the young girls that he desired was really getting to be difficult. He needed to find a way to have his fun without getting caught; he did not want to risk losing his Gina. His sweet and beautiful Gina, who was ten years old, was getting more beautiful every minute. She had inherited his light skin but she also had the exotic looks from her whore mother.

Some of the local political powerhouses had noticed him and wanted to approach him about a career in politics. He was sure it was not only because of his popularity in the school system but also his good looks. After all, he did look like a black Cool Hand Luke and women loved him.

He had been forced to date a few of the single mothers of his students in town, he found them tainted and boring. None of them were virgins and most had long been with many, many, many men. That was a turn off for him; he liked to be their first. But if he was going to get to experience their lovely daughters, he had to first go through them. Once he gained their confidence, getting to their daughters was a piece of cake.

One such mother was the reason why he was leaving teaching to pursue a career in politics.

There was nothing appealing about Lois Winston, a single mother who worked as a secretary at the local high school. She was fat, black, had a whole set of yellow teeth in her mouth, and loud. She had a high school education, and the only subject she knew about was who was sleeping with whom on All My Children. David could not stand the ground she walked on and he would fantasize about killing her each and every time he made love to her.

Her only redeeming attribute was that she had beautiful, thirteen-year-old twin daughters, Bianca and Briana. David loved them on site and encouraged them to come and spend time with Gina whenever they could. He had Lois convinced that they would one day be a family and that the girls needed to spend time together and bond.

Lois, being the lonely woman that she was and grateful that a man like David Ban— only the most handsome black man in Michigan City—was interested in her, let the girls come over. She even let them stay with David when she spent the weekend taking care of her ill mother, who lived in East Chicago.

David could still recall the last time the twins had spent the evening with him and Gina. He remembered because not only was that the night that Gina caught him in the bed with the twins and he had to come up with an excuse for doing so, but it was also the night he knew that he had to change careers.

Gina had retired early after a long night with the twins. She had spent the evening watching horror movies, listening to music, eating pizza and cake, and having the time of her life with the twins, who were going to be her sisters.

After she went to bed, David snuck into the room the twins were using to play their little game. The twins, unlike their mother, were beautiful; and unlike their mother, they knew it. They knew the power that they had over men at an early age and they used it to their advantage.

As David entered the room, the twins were sitting on the bed in the pink panties and t-shirts he liked to see them in. They played the same game every time; let him watch them undress, crawl into bed, let him crawl into bed with them, and fondle them. There was never any sex; they would not permit that. Besides, their mother would check them from time to time to make sure that they were still virgins.

They were well into their game when the door opened and in walked Gina.

"David, what y'all doing? Why are you in the bed with them?"

The twins remained under the covers, and did not say a word but David, who had to think quickly jumped out of bed. Good thing he hadn't taken off his clothes, which was usually part of the game.

"Honey, I was just tucking the girls in bed, and since they were cold, I got in bed with them to warm them up. Now go back to bed, sweetheart, and I will be in there shortly to read to you."

Gina looked at the twins, looked at her brother, and turned to leave. Just as she was going out the door, she turned around again and said, "David, is this what grownups do when they love each other?" That remark scared the hell out of David, who walked with Gina out of the room and down the hall to her room so that the twins would not hear him give Gina the answer he was going to give her.

"Why do you ask that, honey?" David asked, still scared about what she knew.

"Because I was watching cartoons and Foghorn Leghorn told the widow hen, 'I need your love to keep me warm.' Is that what grownups do?"

David was almost in tears at how innocent his "sister" was.

"Yes, Gina, that is what they do, but we are going to make this our little secret, okay. Just between your big brother and you."

"Okay, David." Gina went into her room, got into bed, and wondered why she did not believe her brother.

When David returned to the room where the twins were, they were still undressed and calling their mother to come and pick them up. Bianca was the spokesperson and put the fear in David Ban.

"Mama is coming to pick us up and she is going to be mad about what you have been doing to us."

"What do you mean? Nothing has happened to either one of you."

"But Mama don't know that, and she has a big mouth and will tell the whole town about you if we tell her what you did."

"What the hell do you bitches want?"

"Mama wants to move back to East Chicago to take care of Big Ma and we want to go too. Maybe you can give us the money to move and have enough for us to live off of until Mama finds a job."

"You bitches must be crazy. I ain't giving you or your ugly ass mama any money!"

The doorbell rang and Briana ran out the room butt naked down the hall and opened the door before David could catch her. It was Lois.

"Lois, this is not what you think it is," David said. As he entered the room, Bianca followed him, butt naked as well, "The girls wanted to come home, but I told them not to bother you, sweetheart. I know you are tired from the drive too—wait a minute, I thought you were staying for the weekend?"

"Naw, I came to collect my girls and my money! Oh, David, don't look so surprised. I know what has been going on all this time, I just think it is time to collect. I taught my girls a long time ago how to use what they have to get what they want. I got me some pretty ass babies and I know it; most importantly, they know it too. Go get dressed, girls, the show is over." The girls walked past David with that "boy did we make a fool out of you" look and went back to the room to change. Lois then turned her attention to David. "How about, oh, let's say ten thou—... no, twenty thousand sounds good. That's enough to keep me and my girls from talking and for us to live off of."

David realized that he had been out smarted by a black bitch and her baby bitches. He also knew that if he did not pay, he would go to jail. If that happened, he would lose his position in the city, his money, home, and most of all, his Gina.

He made the check out to Lois Winston for twenty thousand dollars. And decided to leave teaching behind, there must be something else a man with his skills and charisma could do.

That was two months ago and it was the wakeup call for him.

The meeting with the city's powerhouses was to take place at the local restaurant in the city. He did not understand why these powerful men were being so cheap not until he arrived at the restaurant and met with them.

He was led to a table in the back of the restaurant where the three most powerful men, one black two white, sat eating what appeared to be a feast.

Reginald Hampton, who sat in the middle of the other two men, was the richest black man in the city. It was easier to tell people where his money didn't come from because he had his hand into everything, legal and illegal. Reggie, as everyone called him, was also the largest black man David had ever seen. He had to weigh between three and four hundred pounds, with a head shaped like a dolphin, bald as a baby's behind, and at least three chins touching his neck. His eyes looked like round pools of amber and David was surprised that a man with his complexion would have such light colored eyes. He had the nose and mouth of an African slave; both were big, unlike David's, which were more European. His hands were as big as the rest of him, but his fingers were long and rather slender. David almost laughed out loud when he looked down at his feet and found them to be rather small, no more than a size eight. He wondered how the big-ass man could walk and carry all that weight without falling over.

Sitting to Hampton's left was Roy "The Ghost" Karwatka. A much smaller version of Hampton, he was short, thin, and ghost like. However, that was not how he got his nickname. He got the name because he had the ability to enter a room without being noticed; although once he left the room, his presence lingered.

Roy Karwatka was born in the Polish community on Chicago's southeast side but had migrated to Michigan City and had been there for at least thirty years. No one knew anything about his past, and he was not the kind of man to tell. Hampton had once made the mistake of asking the Ghost about the high school he had attended in Chicago, he answered him by making sure that the contract for the high school's new gym went to a rival of Hampton's. Hampton never asked the Ghost anything again. He also brought his reputation with him as a shrewd businessman and a maker of politicians. He had never run for public office, but his name and backing could put a dead man in office ten years after his death.

Unlike Hampton, everyone knew how the Ghost made his money. Real estate; commercial development was where he made his millions. He owned both shopping malls in the city and co-owned two more on the south side of Chicago, the city he would never cut ties with. He still had political allies there since he never knew when those allies would serve to extend his power. But by all appearances, the Ghost was a very simple man.

He lived modestly, unlike Hampton who lived in one of the mansions by Lake Michigan. The Ghost preferred to live across the street from the city's historical cemetery, where he would walk his dog, Lola, every morning and meet with his people to discuss business; the dead never told secrets. Many deals were discussed in that cemetery and business was good.

To Hampton's right sat Sherman O'Malley, head of the leading political party in the county and the ex-police chief of the city. O'Malley had a reputation for being charming, witty and ruthless. His ruthless approach to maintaining law and order in the city made the crime rate one the lowest in the state. But the tactics used by his men had kept the eyebrows raised of most state government officials, including the attorney general. Despite the suspicions, no one could ever prove any wrongdoing on the part of his department under his command.

Even still, he decided to retire from office ten years ago and now made his mark in the political arena. As chairman of his party, nothing got done without his approval—his, and *ultimately, the Ghost's. He knew his star was rising and when the ghost said so, he would move on. He imagined a US Senate seat for himself and he looked forward to a chance to go to Washington.*

These three men sat together eating and enjoying their meals, not knowing that their newest "project" had entered the room and was watching them.

David stood and watched the three men and knew that somehow when he left this meeting, it was going to change his destiny. He was just about to approach them when a hand grabbed his shoulder and the six foot five man attached to that hand stopped him. He was patted down and then escorted to the table.

The Ghost, being the first to see him, turned his attention from Hampton to David. He was the first to speak.

"Mr. Ban, I am Roy, this is Reggie, and this is Sherman, please have a seat. Are you hungry, Mr. Ban? May I call you David? We are all on a first name bases here."

"Yes, David is fine; and yes, I am hungry, thank you." David could feel the power that Roy the Ghost had and sensed that theirs would be a long and interesting relationship.

"Man, Roy, they said this nigga was a Paul Newman look alike! Damn, I ain't ever seen a nigga look like Paul Newman. It was Hampton speaking to the Ghost and the state-ment made David want to pick up the knife that sat to his right and stab that dolphin head son of a bitch. Who the hell was he calling a nigger? And in front of these white men, what the hell was he thinking?

"Boy, sit yo' ass down and enjoy yourself. The food make you want to smack yo' mamma." It was clear Hampton was enjoying his food.

The two men took an instant dislike for each other, which both Sherman and the Ghost noticed and perceived as a positive sign. If things went well, David would be the man they would use; Hampton didn't serve their purpose, not like David would.

It did not take long for the four men to start the discussion of David's future. They wanted him to run for office. There was a state senate seat becoming vacant and it was cur-rently being held by a member of the other party. The trio felt that David's good looks could win the seat, since that district was now becoming populated with more blacks migrating in from Chicago and Detroit.

His face was new and with their backing, he could win the seat. The Ghost asked David if he wanted to take time and sleep on it, but David had heard enough and was ready to make his decision. He would do it. This could lead to bigger and better things.

After the meeting, David drove home to tell Gina about his plans. They were going to be moving in new circles, and he would have to explain to her why that bitch Lois and her baby bitches would not be coming around anymore. Life was going to be good to him and he and his Gina, his love, would live happily ever after.

But before he went home he would stop to see little Maggie Holman. Maggie had been one of his students whose parents had kicked her out when she was fifteen because she was pregnant. Maggie lived in the projects with her five-month-old son and did whatever she had to do to take care of herself and her bastard child. So, if that meant letting David come over once or twice a month for some loving, well, so be it.

The things that girl would do for the $25.00 he left her each time he came by. She even offered to get one of her sisters to come and join the fun, but David had learned his lesson from the bitch twins. No, the needy ones were the best to use, they did not want their money well to run dry.

For the next few weeks, David Ban began his training as the newest political face in the city. The special election was just weeks away and David was up in the polls. He went to every political rally, kissed every snot-nosed baby in his district, shook every hand of every person that came out to support him, all under the watchful eye of The Ghost, O'Malley, and Hampton. Even women voters were impressed with his story of how he was raising his sister Gina alone, but the Ghost insisted that if he were going to have a great political future, he would have to marry. Ideally, it would be someone local; and from one of the best black families in the area.

David did not like the sound of marriage but for his career and for Gina, he would. He needed someone who would look good on his arm, and someone who would be a mother to Gina. He did not want to have anymore children, he had done well having Gina. She was perfect, even if she had the looks of her whore of a mother.

David won the office and was sworn in at the senate chambers to begin his term. The term was short but reelection did not appear to be the problem, as he was the new poster boy for black politicians.

The Ghost and O'Malley celebrated David's victory with a small party for David's staff and a few supporters. Hampton called to say his wife was ill and gave his apologies, but both men knew that Hampton was jealous; he knew his days were numbered. He had made his money, wanted to enter the political arena, but his reputation prevented that. Besides, his kind of skills were needed elsewhere.

They needed someone that could make the blacks in the city do his will, and in turn, they would be doing theirs. David Ban was willing to sell his people down the drain. He really did think he was better than other blacks were, and that was just what they wanted. He would be able to carry out the black migration they had planned. After all, they were experts at picking out the weakest link in the chain, and David Ban was the weakest link.

The next five years were like a whirlwind romance for David politically. He regained his state senate seat and continued to "serve" the people of his district as well as himself and his mentors. When the Ghost decided that the residents of the Edna Pritchett Projects needed to be re-located in order to make room for a shopping mall, townhomes, and condos it was David that helped pass the ordinance. The city then helped hundreds of the tenants move to the west side of the city, and even to the city of Gary, to make way for progress. Of course, the Ghost and his friends made millions off the deal and David was given his thirty pieces of silver for his services.

But the people of his district did not have a clue that he was the "Judas Factor" in their mist. That is because David learned how to play the game and give the people, his so-called people, what they wanted and make his mentors and himself rich in the process.

During his courtship with political life and selling out his people, he met and married the beautiful Glenda Harris. Glenda was born in Michigan City but had spent the last five years in Paris and New York as a runway model. She had returned home to open up spas in the Northwest, Indiana, and Chicago areas. And when David met her, the business was taking off.

She was not the kind of woman David would have picked for himself. First of all, she was dark skinned like his black ass mother had been. But the Ghost thought that her celebrity status would be an asset to him, and the fact that Gina liked her was a plus. If his Gina liked her, the least he could do was marry her.

Of course, he still had his occasional taste for young girls. Maggie, at age nineteen, had gotten too old and used up, so he searched until he found another sweet, pretty, young thing to do his bidding. Maggie had threatened to go to the press about their affair, but the look in David's eyes and the things he said about her body and that of her child's never being found made her think otherwise. And the check that he wrote her for five thousand dollars did a lot for her silence also.

Gina was growing up; and becoming more beautiful every day. She was now fourteen and each day he would look at her and thank God that he had taken both his parents so that he could have Gina to himself. She would stay with him always and he would protect her, no man would ever have her. He would make sure or that.

Glenda and Gina liked each other in the beginning of the marriage, but now things were not so well between theme The main reason for the tension was because Glenda felt that David cared more for Gina than he did her, and she was right.

Also, Glenda wanted to have children of her own, but David wouldn't hear of it. He had his "sister" and that was enough. This made Glenda's resentment of him grow even more, but she liked being Mrs. David Ban and she knew that with the Ghost's help, they were going places. What she did not know was that David had had a vasectomy before the marriage so he would not have to worry about Glenda and any more children.

Yes, life was going well for David and he looked forward to the day when his political career would move forward and he could reach for bigger and better things.

His dead and rotting parents were right in adopting his Gina. He could not imagine life without her. He and that whore Savannah had made one beautiful child, too bad the whore had no clue where her child was. He often wondered what had happened to the whore and her family. He knew that they had moved to Gary, but that was all he knew. Still he wondered what had become of little Miss Savannah Gill.

Chapter 11

Savannah, 1980

Savannah hurried as fast as she could to get home from work. She had to eat and get ready for church quickly or Mama would be furious with her if they were late, and Papa would not speak to her for weeks.

Savannah hated her life. She hated what had become of her after she and the family moved to Gary when she was twelve. Her father would not speak to her, except to make demands, and her mother would always look at her with hurt in her eyes, like it was her fault that she had gotten raped.

The years since she had given birth to her child were not good ones. She was not allowed to watch television, she could only go to school, and do nothing else but attend church. Her father said that she would have to atone for her sin for the rest of her life and that he would make sure that she did just that.

Despite the fact that she had no friends in school, Savannah did well; and in her senior year, won a full scholarship to attend college in another state.

Her father and mother said no. And so, after graduation, Savannah found a job at the local school and worked in the cafeteria as a lunch matron. She was miserable, but her father said that after what she had done to the family, that was what she deserved.

For years, her parents punished her for what had happened to her at age eleven. Even Nana had tormented her saying that she must have done something to encourage David to do what he did, just like Eve tempted Adam in the Bible to eat of the forbidden fruit.

Now at age twenty, Savannah was getting restless and she wanted to move on with her life, but she had no one to help her and she feared that no help would come. But Savannah continued to pray for a way out and that God would help her to be content with her life until he opened another door for her to walk in.

She arrived at home on time, washed up, ate, and waited in the car for Mama and Nana to come out so that they could ride to church together. They went to church at least five times a week, and had two services on Sunday. Since Papa was the district bishop, he was expected to visit churches on a regular basis and tend to the two he had, one in Gary and one in Benton Harbor, Michigan. That meant going to Michigan every other Sunday and Savannah hated making that trip. Her father would ignore her for most of the trip he and Nana and Mama would discuss church affairs and they would always return home late Sunday night, just in time for bed and the whole weekly routine to start over again on Monday.

Tonight, they were going to hear Bishop Carlton Stokes speak at the Stokes Temple Church of God Devine on 87th and Ontario in Chicago. Bishop Stokes was fifty-four years old and had recently lost his wife. Rumor had it that he was looking for a Godly woman to replace his wife and that the women in the area were waging all-out war to be the next first lady of his church.

Savannah felt sorry for those ladies, how sad to live your life wanting to be at the beck and call of your husband. That was not the kind of life that she wanted for herself. She wanted to live her life by her own rules, God's and hers of course, but she just did not see it happening.

They arrived at the church just in time and settled in for the evening's worship service. After church was over and they were going out the door, Savannah heard a voice calling her and at first did not realize who it was until her called her name again. That is when she realized that it was her father calling her. His voice was so soft and pleasant that she did not recognize he was speaking to her. He had never spoken to her in that tone, it was always harsh and cruel.

As she turned to walk toward her father, she saw Bishop Stokes looking at her and a cold feeling came over her. Papa introduced her to the bishop and pointed out how pretty she was. He said she had not been exposed to the world, too much anyway, and then invited the bishop over to dinner at their house the following evening. That is when she knew what her father was up to. He wanted to marry her off to this man; this man who looked at her with lust in his eyes and she knew the time had come for her to make her move.

The next day at work, Savannah talked with her boss about a position in the school as a paraprofessional that she wanted to apply for. Her boss had always encouraged her to apply for any and every position that became available. She did not like the fact that Savannah was wasting her life in a job that would lead to nothing. She knew how smart

Savannah was but she also knew that Savannah would have to realize it too and do something about it.

So, when Savannah asked the boss about the position, not only did she give Savannah permission to apply online, she wrote her a letter of recommendation.

That night at dinner, as her father, mother, Nana, and Bishop Stokes discussed her future as if she were not there, Savannah sat there and made her own plans. She was going to get that job, move out, go to school, and get a degree; she did not know in what, but she was going to get one.

A week later, Savannah received a call about her application for the position, and set up an interview time for the following day.

She borrowed clothes from her friend Regina, who worked with her and wore the same size as Savannah. There was no way she could dress like that and leave home, not without Nana and Mama questioning her, and she did not want them to know.

The interview went so well, the letter from her boss being the icing on the cake, that she was offered the job with a five dollar per hour raise. Savannah accepted the position, as well as the fact that she would now have to have a showdown with her family if she was ever going to live her life.

She was to start in a week. Her current boss had agreed to release her, and now she needed to buy clothes that would be appropriate for her new job. She was going to tell her parents and Nana the day before the job started but would wait until she got an apartment before she told them she was going to move out.

She also decided to go against her parents' teachings, and her faith, and wear pants. So when she shopped for new clothes, she would buy pants. She discovered that she had a cute little shape and when she took her hair down, she was beautiful. Her hair was down to her waist, her father had not allowed her to cut it, and now she decided that if she were going to be the new Savannah, the hair would have to go too.

Her new look happened on the Saturday before she was going to make her big announcement. Regina, her friend at work, had recommended a beautician who could do wonders with her hair. So Saturday morning, Savannah went to him and let him have his way with her hair. He cut it about an inch past her shoulders and gave her the first perm she had ever had in her life. The ninety-five dollars she paid was worth it! She loved her new look. In about two weeks, she was going to come back so that he could put some color in it.

After getting her hair done, Savannah went shopping for new clothes, shoes, and a purse. She bought three pairs of pants, tops, shoes that were comfortable as well as fashionable, and a Coach purse, her first. She had money to spend. Her father had made her give him half of her salary when she started working, and she had saved the rest; not spending money on much, a magazine every once in a while that she had to sneak into the house.

Nana made all of her clothes, and they were horrible. She dressed her like a matron with all of her dresses and skirts falling well below her knees, some almost to her ankles.

Now she was going to wear pants, she would dress in her dresses at home and change when she got to work. She was excited about the new job and the new direction she was taking in her life, but she was scared to death about having to face her family about her decision. If only her cussing angel Gemini were around for support. She knows that Gemini would have cussed all three of her family members out and would take her by the hand and leave.

Savannah wondered through the years how Gemini was doing. She wondered about the babies they had both given birth to and wondered where they were. Although Gemini lived in the same city, they had not run into each other over the years. Maybe God knew best, but she wanted to see her so badly. She wanted to discuss their past, what their lives had been like up until now, and if Gemini often thought about her own child, as Savannah did.

She had been hearing a lot about David Ban and the mark he was making in politics in his city. She saw pictures of him in the newspapers and read stories about how much the citizens in his city loved him. She cried the first time she saw Gina in the paper with him. Then marveled at how beautiful she was and hoped that one day they would be united. She knew that Ban was raising her as his sister, but she knew that, somehow, the truth would come out.

One day when she got herself together, she would find Gina, make her acquaintance, and they would become friends; that was the least that she could hope for.

Sunday came, the big day when Savannah was going to make her big announcement. She would start by showing them her hair. Her father always insisted that she wear her hair covered in public, but this Sunday she was not. She took the scarf off after getting dressed for church, combed her hair, and looked in the mirror. She decided then that she would buy and start to wear makeup once she moved out on her own.

Nana, Mama, and Papa were already downstairs eating when Savannah entered the room. At first, they did not even notice her, but the minute she sat down, Nana was the first to notice.

"Lord have mercy, Savannah Marie Gill! What have you done to your hair?" Nana screamed. "Get back upstairs and cover your hai—... oh, my God, you cut your hair... you cut your hair!"

This statement caused her parents to look up and gasp at the same time. Her mother just stared at her as if she had just stepped off a space ship and her father looked at her with a disgust that she had never seen before.

"This is my new look and I will not be covering my hair anymore. I like the way I look, it is a look that will go with the new job that I start tomorrow. I have interviewed and accepted the position as a paraprofessional at the school. I will be helping the first grade teacher, Mrs. Ferrell, with her class. They are paying me eleven dollars an hour. Please, all of you be happy for me. I am doing what I feel is my calling to help young children." The courage she was experiencing must have come from God because she continued to tell them her plans. "I am also planning to find an apartment which I will move into in a few months. It is time that I take a step out into the world. I am twenty years old and I feel as if I have lived in a cave all my life. I feel that the three of you have never let me forget what happened to me when I was eleven, but it was not my fault. God has helped me to realize that. It is not my sin to bear, and I am tired of being made to feel that it is."

No one spoke for a few seconds and then her father said something she half expected him to say, but the words still hurt just the same.

"Get out; get out of my house now!" Rev Gill jumped up; and before anyone could stop him, he was grabbing Savannah and forcing her out the dining room and to the front door. Savannah kicked, screamed, and begged her father to stop. He would have succeeded too if her mother hadn't raised her voice and stopped him.

"Earl Gill, take your hands off her! I said leave her alone!" The force of her words was so powerful that it stopped him dead in his tracks. When Nana, who had started praying every prayer she had in her repertoire, started to rise in protest to support her son, Leona Gill stopped her dead in her tracks too.

"Sit down, Mother Gill, this is not your fight; this is between Savannah, her father, and me." There was an edge to her voice that made Nana sit down immediately.

"How dare you talk to me that way," Earl Gill spat out to his wife. He didn't know who he was angrier at, Savannah or his wife who was speaking out of turn."

"I dare because I have been married to you for twenty-five years and I have let you create a hell for my baby and I did nothing to stop you. Well, that is over. Now take your hands off my baby or I will sing it from every church in the district what a Godless, evil man you really are, you hypocrite!"

By this time she had made her way to her husband and was standing directly in his face, daring him with her eyes to make a move. Savannah had never noticed until this moment that her mother was slightly taller than her father by at least an inch. During the faceoff, Savannah eased from the grip that her father had on her and stood next to her mother. Her father looked defeated now and what he did next surprised even Savannah, he went back to his seat and sat down.

Leona Gill looked in her daughter's eyes and with one swift movement, fell to her knees. She was crying and holding on to Savannah's hem, and the sight of her kneeling at Savannah's feet brought tears to Savannah's eyes.

"Baby girl, I want you to forgive me. Forgive me, Savannah, for not being the mother that you needed when you needed me most. You were just eleven years old when that man raped you and you have had to endure the hell your father, grandmother, and I put you through all these years. I was afraid, baby girl; afraid to face what happened; afraid that I would not know how to comfort you; and afraid that we all failed to protect you. I was not angry at you, sweetness, I was mad at myself and God, yes, God, for making you go through what you did. But I have watched you grow into a wonderful person and I know that you have made it through the storm with God's help while the rest of us are still in the midst of it. Your father and Nana are also mad with themselves for what happened to you. That's why I am asking you for forgiveness, for me as well as for your father and grandmother. Can you find it in your heart?" She was crying uncontrollably now and to help her, Savannah got down on her knees and did to her mother what her mother should have done to her when she was eleven. She comforted her.

And that is how Savannah Gill entered her new life, a life full of promise, hope, and most of all, forgiveness.

Savannah took to her new job like a duck to water; it was as if the job were created just for her. She was assigned to assist Mrs. Joplin with her second grade class. She and her "teacher" hit it off immediately and the children loved her. It was bitter sweet for Savannah, for she loved children and longed to have more, but she often thought about her own little girl.

Her job was to assist the teacher with class projects and to act as a sort of observer for the children and to report to Mrs. Joplin anything that she felt needed Mrs. Joplin's immediate attention. The school day was from 8:00 a.m. to 3:00 p.m., which worked out great for her because she could go shopping, have an early dinner with Regina, and still get home in time to attend church with her parents and Nana. She did not, however, go five times a week like she used to in the past. She was a new, independent person and she liked the things that her new job and her new outlook on life had to offer.

Most of the time, she and her friend Regina would hang out and go to dinner, or the movies, which she could never tell her father or Nana she was going to. And now she was considering taking aerobics lessons. Aerobics was becoming popular in the Midwest and there were classes being held in different parts of the city.

Of course, she would never tell her father or Nana what she was doing but, surprisingly, her mother wanted to know how she was enjoying her new life. Sometimes the two of them would go out for lunch on Saturday's and she would tell her mother about her week, the job, the students, her teacher, her friend Regina, and the places they went to for dinner. One day she decided to tell her mother about going to the movies and was surprised when her mother said that one of the things she missed was going to the movies. She used to go with her friends when she was younger, before she married the Bishop. She even remembered the last movie she saw before she got married; it was The Good, The Bad and The Ugly with Clint Eastwood and Lee van Cleef. She encouraged Savannah to continue to have fun and promised that her new life would be their secret; her father must never know, or Nana for that matter.

When Savannah brought up the subject of school, her mother said she would do everything she could to help. She wanted her baby to have the life that she felt she had been denied by her self-righteous husband and bitter mother-in-law; and, of course, a mother who had been too scared to defy her husband, being the good, God-fearing woman that she was. She prayed to God every night for forgiveness and hoped that one day he would.

After six months, Savannah had saved up enough money to move into an apartment. She thought it best to move out on her own and not share an apartment with anyone, especially Regina. It wasn't that she didn't think that she could live with Regina; she was worried that if things did not work out, she would lose a friend.

She announced her decision to move at Sunday dinner. Her father had said little to her in the six months since she announced her new life. He did his talking from the pulpit; ranting and raving about lost souls and how God would punish the ungodly. He preached about how the world corrupts and tempts young people and how those who stepped out into the world to do the devil's work, would see fire and hell in the hereafter. Savannah knew that most of his messages were directed toward her, but she didn't care, she had made her peace with God.

Nana did most of her talking with her friends. She talked about her only grandchild behind her back, and that did not sit well with her daughter-in-law, who politely told Nana about herself one Sunday morning at breakfast. The Bishop came to his mother's defense but was quickly shot down by the new and improved Leona Gill. She had never stood up to her husband, but in recent months, as she saw her daughter grow and develop into the kind of woman that she herself had always wanted to be, Leona was determined that her daughter was going to live the life that she deserved. Damn her husband and his mama.

The day that Savannah moved, it rained. Her father told her it was God's way of telling her that her decision would bring her nothing but sorrow.

"Just like how being raped at eleven and having you blame me all my life filled my life with sorrow?" Savannah responded in anger at her father's statement.

She was not afraid of her father anymore, and was looking forward to making her way in the world. She would show the old self-righteous hypocrite, she would show her Nana too. It would be the best revenge, the sweetest revenge. Success; Savannah Gill was on a mission.

Savannah excelled in her new life, first the job, then college for a degree in Social Work; she wanted to help other rape victims like herself. Then she completed her master's in Social Work, which led her to work at several agencies dedicated to helping women and families. But Savannah wanted to start her own agency, so after a few years of learning the ins and outs of social work and a lot of grant writing, Savannah was able to open her own social service agency, which she named "Highly Favored," a name her mother helped her to come up with.

Highly Favored was an agency dedicated to helping victims of domestic violence, rape, and drug abuse, as well as help adults obtain their GEDs. The agency's faith-based approach helped families through counseling, job placement, and other supportive services. Savannah's whole life became seeing to the comfort of others and her name as a woman of compassion was well known in the city. For one, people were impressed by how young she was, not even thirty and yet she had one of the most successful social service agencies in the area. The agency had some of the most successful citizens in the city as contributors and the agency was able to expand within a few years. Her success made her the guest of many universities in the area and she was talked into conducting a class on social work at one of them as a visiting instructor.

During the time that all of this took place, Savannah saw little of her mother and her father. Nana had passed away the year before, but not before she had her talk with Savannah. She never asked for forgiveness, rather she told Savannah how proud she was of her, but that making her way back to God would be the only way she could redeem herself. That meant going back to church and re-establishing her faith in God. It was no use trying to convince Nana that she had never left God; that she had chosen to serve God in a manner that was more suited for her, so she just listened and nodded. Nana passed peacefully in her sleep with Savannah and her parents by her side.

Her father never came to terms with any of Savannah's decisions, even as she became more successful and expanded the agency to include an adult daycare center and was making plans to offer an after school program for latchkey kids; yet, her father never said more than a few words to her. Her mother was a different story. Each day after work, she would call her mother and let her know how her day was, who she was seeing, how the agency was *doing, the house that she was looking to buy, all of this she told to her mother. They had become almost like girlfriends, laughing and talking on the phone each night, confiding in each other, and enjoying each other. They even discussed the baby and what she might be doing now. Savannah knew where her daughter was, she was still living with her father/ brother, but she wondered if she would ever see her child.*

Once while reading the paper during a break from classes, she stumbled on an article about a case involving a woman accused of trying to kill her boss. The man had been beaten with an award on his desk. The accused was a woman who was bipolar and it was discovered by her attorney that the woman needed to have her medicine changed. Savannah almost jumped out of her skin when she read the name of the attorney. It was her old friend, Gemini Jones.

Chapter 12

We were still waiting for Bookie to tell us what happened.

"My sources tell me that the district 'assttorney' is holding a press conference today to announce the arrests of several police officers who have been working for Quentin 'Shorty' Hanes, the drug dealer. Seems they have been stealing evidence out of the evidence room which meant that Shorty and his people were walking on a lot of charges. The shit has hit the shield, so to speak."

"And what does that have to do with Savannah's case," I asked, still trying to figure out what the hell Bookie was talking about.

"Well, it seems that in the course of getting rid of the shit that would put Shorty away, one of the dumb asses mistakenly got rid of the gun in Savannah's case. The DA is pissed beyond pissosity!"

"Holy shit, somebody up there likes us," Israel said in response to Bookie's news. "No gun, no TV crew got footage on her shooting Ban, what more could a person accused of murder want?"

"Bookie, are you sure about this? I mean, this is big and if it's true then you're right, that is the reason why the DA wants to call us in for a plea bargain!"

"As sure as you are three people, all my Gemini. There is going to be a press conference held this afternoon after he meets with you."

The meeting with the DA took place a few hours later. Omar Robinson had to be the most handsome, arrogant bastard that ever came out of a woman in birth. He was six foot three, blacker than ten midnights, and fine as hell. He worked out every day, played in a jazz band when he had the time, took his mother to church every Sunday, and was being considered as a candidate for governor.

Still, he was the biggest asshole in the city. I could not stand him personally, but he was effective and voters had told him so twice.

The meeting took place in his office. Savannah was still in the hospital, so I had to go alone.

Entering his office was like entering a shrine to himself. Every award he had been given since elementary school was placed on the wall. His law degree from Harvard; his awards for service from the mayor and the governor; his letter from President Reagan and a letter from basketball great Joe "The Eagle" Reigle, for his putting away the men who had murdered Reigle's brother two years earlier.

He greeted me with his famous "shake you like churning butter" handshake and invited me to sit down.

"How is Ms. Wooten doing? I have her report here on my desk; it doesn't look good."

"Then you know how she is. What is this about, Omar?"

"As you know I have a pretty good case against your client, but now that I know she is terminally ill, I am willing to plea bargain. I don't want a terminally ill woman spending the rest of her life in prison. And it does not look good for me to pick on a sick woman, even if she did kill one of the most loved politicians in the state."

"Make me an offer, Omar," I said, confident that what Bookie had told me earlier was a sure thing. "However, before you do, can you confirm or deny a rumor I heard?"

Omar Robinson did not make it to the DA office being stupid. He knew that I had something and that I was ready to use it.

"What is it Gemini?"

"I hear from a reliable source that you are holding a press conference this afternoon because your office has just indicted some crooked cops after some evidence has come up missing in the Quentin Hanes case; is that true?"

Omar knew where this was headed, and he didn't like it one bit.

"You have good sources, or should I say Bookie Lyman has good sources."

"Then you know my next question, but I will ask anyway. By any chance in the course of getting rid of the Hanes evidence, did they mistakenly get rid of the gun that killed David Ban?"

"It appears that several pieces of evidence are missing from a lot of cases, my office is working closely with the police to ascertain what is missing."

"I know I look like Boo Boo T. Fool, Omar. I know I walk, talk, and act like Boo Boo T. Fool, but Boo Boo T. Fool I am not. The gun in my client's case is missing and you don't have a case, you don't have film footage, your witnesses are questionable, and now the gun is missing. From where I sit, you don't have jack shit and you want me to bargain?"

"My witnesses can put the gun at Ms. Wooten's feet, the rest is circumstantial."

"What is the motive?" I was anxious to hear what he had to say and scared at the same time.

"It appears that Ban rejected your client's advances on several occasions, that she came to his house numerous times; and that six months before she killed him in prime time, she was at his home and there was a heated argument between them. She did not have any respect for the fact that Ban had just buried his sister, Gina."

"So, is that why Ban's wife invited Savannah to the press conference, to continue the argument they had months earlier? Come on, Omar, I won't rent that piece of bullshit, let alone buy it! You have got to do better than that."

"I am. By offering you 'man one,' she serves what little time she has left in jail."

"And you want to do a threesome with me and Halle Berry; but that isn't going to happen either."

I knew Omar did not like my response, he found it to be so ghetto, which is really what he thought of me; just another black woman raised from nothing who got into law school because of affirmative action and became a lawyer. Unlike himself, who was born into a very wealthy black family, his father owned an insurance company in Chicago and several other businesses and even owned part of the Chicago Grizzlies franchise. Omar Robinson was one of these brothas who looked down on people. You were only as good as the money you made or your family background.

"Don't let this go to trial, Gemini. You are going to lose, and Ms. Wooten has suffered enough."

"On the contrary, Omar. I think I have a good chance of getting my client off. Anyone could have shot Ban and threw the gun at Savannah's feet. None of the film crews got coverage of the actual shooting and your witnesses place the gun at her feet, not in her hand. And now that the gun is missing, well, I say the cards are stacked against you; not my client."

"Gemini, there is no way in hell I am going to let your client walk, someone has to pay for Ban's death and from where I am sitting, that would be your client. She had motive and opportunity, and she did confess to the police."

"Funny, I don't remember my client signing anything. I heard that she may have said something incriminating to the police but even that is questionable. After all, your office did put the pressure on to find something on my client, maybe one of the police were overzealous and thought my client said something about killing Ban. Who is really sure?" I felt confident that I had Robinson by the balls and I was squeezing as hard as I could.

"Then I guess we will be going to trial." Omar sat back in his chair, anyone who knew him or had dealings with him knew that when he leaned back into his chair, he was bluffing. "No, I am preparing a motion to have the charges dismissed on my client, even as we speak, and it will come right after you announce that the murder weapon in my client's case is missing."

"That could take days for that press conference to take place."

"Oh, I am sure it will take place today, or I will have one of my own."

"See you in court, Gemini." He had that "you're dismissed" tone in his voice, which irritated the hell out of me.

"And I will see you in Judge Adams's office when I bring in my motion to dismiss all the charges against my client."

I got up and left his office.

I decided to stop by and see Savannah before I went back to the office. She was still in the infirmary and I almost cried at the sight of her.

In the weeks since she had been arrested, she seemed to have aged twenty years. Her skin looked as if it was shrinking from her body, it was almost as if the cancer knew of her situation and was trying to finish her off quick.

She was barely awake when I sat down next to her bed. Morphine had become her best friend and her speech was slow and slurred.

"There's my cussin' angel. Hey, Gemini, how's my attorney doing today?"

"A whole lot better than you are right now. Damn, Savannah, I cannot stand to see you like this. Why am I fighting so hard for you and you won't fight for yourself?"

"Because you always protected me and that is something that you can't seem to stop. But I would not have it any other way."

"Well, I do have some news that will make you feel better. My sources tell me that the district attorney is going to have a press conference today to announce the arrest of some crooked cops who have been destroying evidence for some big drug dealer. It seems that in the course of destroying evidence for him, they destroyed the gun that was used to kill David."

I looked at her to get a reaction. All I got was the sound of her snoring.

Back at the office, my team was meeting in my office to listen to the press conference of District Attorney Robinson. Bookie was not in the office and was on an assignment for the firm.

I came in just in time to see DA Robinson come up to the mikes and make his opening statement.

"As you all know, my office has been investigating the dealings of accused drug lord Quentin 'Shorty' Hanes. During this investigation into his illegal participation in the distribution and sale of crack cocaine, it was discovered that key pieces of evidence have turned up missing from the evidence room at police headquarters. After several months, the special task force, along with internal affairs, have compiled enough evidence to arrest and indict six policemen who have had a long affiliation with Hanes. The officers are: Manuel Costas, a twenty-year veteran; Julius James, a eighteen-year veteran; Kevin Weathers, a fourteen-year veteran; Ruth Loggins, who is the daughter of retired police chief Warren Summers, and Christopher Connolly, both served ten years on the force. They have all been arrested and charged with, among other things, conspiracy to distribute and sell crack cocaine. They will also be charged with the hampering of an on- going police investigation, although that is the least of their worries. We are also looking into the murders of several of Hanes's competitors, including that of his alleged mentor, Amahl Malik Williams; known on the street as 'the Saint.' Further charges should be coming from my office in the next few weeks. We are also looking into the possibility that other evidence not associated with Hanes and his organization was destroyed. I will now take questions."

We did not see the person who asked the first question but I recognized the voice; it was Shannon Bradley, a reporter for one of the Chicago papers. She asked the question that I had hoped would get asked first.

"District Attorney Robinson, is it true that one of the pieces of evidence destroyed was the gun that killed senator Ban?"

The look on Robinson's face was a look of sheer shock. He had not been prepared to have that question put to him, which shocked me because I knew that he knew that the information had been leaked to Bookie and the team. Did he not realize how fast news like that travelled?

"I cannot say at this time what evidence has been destroyed other than that belonging to the Hanes case. We will be keeping you posted as this case develops."

"But, District Attorney Robinson, isn't it true that you already know that the gun in that case was destroyed, which is why you had a meeting today with

Savannah Wooten's attorney, Gemini Jones, to discuss a plea bargaining?" Bradley shot back.

Everyone in my office reacted the same way. We all sat up straight in our seats and yelled, "Oh, shit!" How did she know about the meeting and who from my office or Robinson's office would tell the press? I had not even had the motion to withdraw the indictment drawn up yet. Then I remembered something and it all came together. She had been one of Bookie's women a long time ago; as a matter of fact she was the only woman who had ever broken his heart. Could he have leaked that information to her? I wondered, and made a mental note to ask him when he got back to the office.

"Do you think that we will have a chance that the judge will throw it out?" Ismael asked. "They have nothing; N-O-T-H-I-N-G!"

"Damn, Ish, I did not know you could spell," Bookie said as he walked into my office. Hey, all my Gemini, did you see the district assttorney on the tube? Loved that suit he had on, did not like the tie."

"Where did you see his suit, Bookie?" I asked, but I already knew the answer the moment the question came out of my mouth.

"At the press conference, of course. I watched it on TV just like everyone else."

"Yeah right, sure your ass did," I snapped back. "You were there and you leaked that information to Shannon Bradley, didn't you?" I was getting pissed that he would do such a thing and my team felt my anger. One by one they quietly left the office. As Ish was leaving, I told him to prepare my motion to have the charges against Savannah dismissed and leave it on my desk before he left for the evening. I turned back to Bookie without skipping a beat.

"Leaking is something that you do when your adult diaper gets too full of pee. Now, what I did was add a little leverage to the game. When the press gets through with Robinson and the police force for what happened, the district assttorney will be dropping the charges against a whole lot of people who caught a case. I just hope that Savannah Wooten is one of them."

"You had no right to do that without running it by me first!" I was angry at him and I really did not know why.

"Okay, who am I talking with now, is it Gemini, her evil twin Kremini, or do you have another person inside there that I have not met yet?"

"You are not an attorney, and I am not a private detective. I do not cross your boundaries, and I do not expect you to cross mine."

"But you do expect me to jump through hoops and roll over and play dead, is that what all y'all want? What in the hell is eating at y'all?" Then, with a boyish look in his eye, he said, "Why Gemini, are you jealous that I spent time with Shannon?" That grin he had on his face as he left my office did not bother me, what he had just said did. Because he was right, I was jealous.

Yes, it was true, I did have feelings for Bookie; and he knew it, we just never discussed it. I know that he has feelings for me; again, we never discussed it.

If it were up to him, we probably would have had some sort of affair a long time ago, but I just could not bring myself to do it. Why? Because I was scared as hell, I did not trust myself to make the right decisions when it came to love and romance. As much as I wanted it, I was afraid that when it finally made its way to me, somehow I would mess things up. I had a lifetime of hurt and I had enough baggage to start my own luggage company.

The press was starting to call my office for my reaction to today's press conference. I told Antoinette to inform them that I had no comments yet. I wanted to set up another meeting with Omar to discuss my motion for dismissal.

I wanted to speak to Bookie. I wanted to explain my outburst. It was not my illness speaking, it was my heart, my fear and my heart, both working at the same time. Both trying hard not to drive him away but knowing that if I kept things the way that they were, I would do the one thing I did not want to do. And that was to drive a wedge between the two of us. I knew that I would have to face these feeling that I had for him and deal with it.

But first things first, I had to get my client out of jail and back at home so that she could die in peace.

I was on my way to see Savannah again, I just wanted to check on her and let her know about the motion that I was filing.

She seemed to be worse each time that I saw her. The past few weeks in jail and cancer had taken its toll on her.

She was fully awake when I walked in. "Hey, cussing angel, I'm so sorry that I went to sleep on you on your last visit. The morphine keeps me that way. And I can give it to myself," she said as she pointed to the morphine pump. "What can I do for you today?"

"You can tell me what happen with you and Ban. The police think that you had an affair with him and that you killed him because he would not leave his wife. What happened, Savannah; what happened between you and Ban? I know you said that he killed Gina, but that is not true. According to the police report, she committed suicide."

"He killed her, Gemini. He killed her and was not even in the room when it happened. He killed her well before she took her own life."

Chapter 13

(One Year and eight months before David Ban went to his ancestors.)

Highly Favored had now become one of the most successful agencies in the state and the founder, Savannah Wooten, was the force behind the success. She now concentrated her efforts on speaking engagements and charity events on behalf of the agency. After all, money was needed and there was plenty of money to be gotten.

During this time, Savannah met and married George Wooten, a local businessman whose mother had been the victim of domestic violence when he was a boy. The union was a good one but ended suddenly when George was killed in a car accident shortly after leaving work one evening. His estate went to Savannah and his grown children. Savannah used her portion to run Highly Favored and continued her speaking engagements to help with her loss.

On one occasion, Savannah was invited to speak at a women's group on the effects of domestic violence. As she drove to Michigan City for the event, her heart was filled with joy, and a little sadness. For some reason she had been thinking about her daughter a lot in the past few days and the sadness that she felt was unbearable. However, she knew that there was work to be done, so she decided to hire a private investigator to check on Gina and let her know how her daughter was doing. Gina was grown by now and still living with Ban and his wife, Glenda. She would see Gina standing next to him at some event they were on attending on television; Ban was a very popular politician, thanks to the Ghost and his cronies. Ban was making a bid for the governorship and Savannah wanted the world to know just what a monster he really was, but she knew that if she came forward, it would hurt Gina. She could not afford for that to happen.

The women's conference was held at the newly found Women's Center in Michigan City, a center which Ban had founded. How ironic that she was going to speak to a group of women on abuse in the center founded by the man who had abused her. Life was hard, but God was good. Something good could come from all of this.

She was greeted at the center by Glenda Ban and her assistant, Greta. Glenda was as beautiful in person as she was on TV and in the magazines. But there was a sadness in her eyes, and Savannah could only surmise that it had to do with the man that she was married to.

"Ms. Wooten, it is a pleasure to have you here today," Glenda said as she walked up and hugged Savannah. This is my assistant, Greta, she will be assisting you today. If you need anything, Ms. Wooten, you just let Greta know and it will be taken care of."

"You can start by calling me Savannah," Savannah replied, "and I am very happy to be here." It was at that point in the conversation that she noticed the look on Glenda's face had changed from one of joy to one of anger. She seemed to be looking over Savannah's shoulder and the look on her face was so intense that it made Savannah turn around to see the source of such a change.

And that is when she saw what had made Glenda so angry but had made her heart jump for joy. Savannah found it hard to contain her excitement, fear, and all the other emotions that she was feeling.

Gina and the nicest looking young man she had seen in ages were approaching them. She was finally going to meet her daughter.

Gina Ban was a vision, as beautiful as an angel, and walked with an air that made people take another look at her. Not only for her beauty, but for the way she seemed to light up a room when she walked in. It was like God had sent the best of his crew down on Earth to walk among the mortals to let the world know that he had sent his best to watch over them.

Savannah was surprised to see that Gina favored her grandmother. Boy would Nana have been surprised had she known, but Nana had died the year before without ever coming to terms with her relationship with her only grandchild. Her hair was long, way past her shoulders, and was the prettiest shade of golden brown. Her eyes where the color of Lake Michigan during a rain storm, a sort of deep gray with just a hint of green. She was not tall but her back was straight and that gave her a tall appearance. She was well dressed, but not overly, and although her clothes were tight, it revealed a body that Savannah recognized so well. She was built like her!

She and her male friend made their way to Savannah and Glenda, and Gina held out her hand to Savannah.

"Hi, Ms. Wooten, I'm Gina Ban and this is my boyfriend, Ronny Washington. I have heard so much about you and have even attended some of your lectures at the university. I am planning on getting my undergraduate in Child Development and my masters in Social Work. Then, I plan to open an agency just like Highly Favored. I really do like that name, why did you choose it?"

"Because I am highly favored," Savannah replied, "knowing that you are well **and standing here in front of me looking as beautiful as I knew you would be**, and I want the people who come to my agency for help to feel the same way."

Ronny spoke next. "Ms. Wooten, all Gina ever talks about is you. She is so impressed with you that I had to break an engagement that we were invited to just to come and meet the woman my lady is so smitten with."

That made Savannah want to jump for joy, take Gina by the hand, and announce to the world who Gina was. But she could only respond to Ronny's statement.

"I am flattered by all of this, and truly humbled. Thank you for the compliment. I hope you're coming here was not an inconvenience."

"You know you do not have to stay for the whole event, Gina," Glenda said. Savannah could tell by the way that Glenda spoke she really did not want Gina and Ronny there. She seemed to resent Gin; and that is when Savannah realized what Ban had done. He had married Glenda to be a mother for Gina, and maybe for her money, but there was no love in that marriage and she knew it. The only love he seemed to have was for Gina. And that made Savannah afraid.

"Glenda, if it is all the same to you, I want to stay. Besides, Ronny really does want to go to that party at the country club and I don't want to stop him from having fun. But I really want to stay and hear Ms. Wooten." Gina appeared to be oblivious to the resentment that Glenda had for her, she really appeared to like Glenda.

"Please, call me Savannah, all of my friends do," Savannah said, making an effort to become her friend.

"All right, Savannah, I will stay. But first let me get my man on the road to his party. I will be joining you later. There is so much that I want to discuss with you."

"I will be right here, Gina," Savannah said. She wanted to grab her hand and kiss it, but she just stood there, cool and collected.

"It was nice meeting you, Ms. Wooten," Ronnie said as he shook her hand.

Savannah liked this young man and it was obvious that they were in love.

"That goes for you too, Ronny, please call me Savannah. And it was really nice to meet you as well."

She watched the two lovebirds walk away hand in hand and there was joy in her heart. At least her little girl was happy and that made all the suffering of her past worth it. But as she turned to say something to Glenda, the look on Glenda's face made her cringe. It was the look of sheer hatred.

A few days after first meeting with Gina, she received a call from her with an offer to have lunch with her and Ronny at a sports bar of one of Ronny's teammates. Savannah accepted and they agreed to meet the next day at R.I.P.'s Sports Bar. The bar was located across the street from a cemetery and despite the location, was actually one of the most popular places in Michigan City. Ronny lived in Chicago but his teammate, Simeon Gray, was from Michigan City and, like Ronny, had signed a multimillion dollar deal with the Bears. Also like Ronny, he had started several businesses in his hometown. Ronny was from Marion and had done the same thing. Savannah wondered if he knew anything about Mamie Wells's home but decided not to ask.

They had lunch with Ronny the following day and dinner the day after that. Weeks of meeting for lunch and dinner turned into months of meeting, and it looked as if Gina and Savannah were going to be friends. Savannah had not expected that much, but was grateful that she could be a part of Gina's life.

Their relationship had made them close, so much so that when Savannah was invited to go to New York to speak, she invited Gina to come along. They spent several days there and had the time of their lives. Gina had finally found someone that she could get close to; Savannah was like an older sister, someone she could trust. Savannah liked the fact that her daughter had wanted to be her friend; had come to rely on her and trust her.

Savannah really liked Ronny Washington. Although he was one of the best athletes in football and had the money to prove it, he was down to earth and really loved Gina. They had met a year ago through a mutual friend, who thought that Ronny could use someone special in his life. Ronny was still thanking the friend every time they saw each other.

Gina often confided in Savannah about her family. Both of her parents had died in a car accident when she was seven and she had been raised by her brother, David, and her sister-in-law, Glenda. Glenda and David had no children of their own, which made Gina sad because she thought that Glenda would have made a wonderful mother and maybe if she had a child of her own, she would not be so indifferent to Gina.

Savannah would sit and listen to Gina talk about how over protective David was to her. He had never wanted her to go off to school; instead, he paid for her to attend college in the area. He did not like Ronny Washington but would never explain to Gina the reason. He was just an over protective brother who did not want her to have any close friends, which was why she had not told him about Savannah at least not just yet. She was going to wait until she felt the moment was right.

She assured Savannah that although David was a little strange, he was not crazy for not wanting her to have friends. He explained that in his arena, they were sitting targets for all kinds of scandal and he did not want that sort of mess to come into their lives.

Savannah did not reply to what Gina told her, but it did leave a sick feeling in the bottom of her stomach. David Ban had a sickness for young girls and she was afraid that his feelings for Gina were not normal; but David Ban was not normal. She would stay around Gina for as long as she could. She would protect her baby at all cost.

Two months after she began her friendship with Gina, Ronny asked Gina to marry him. He had gone to Savannah and had asked her advice on the best way to propose. He wanted it to be the most special moment for Gina, but as a man, he did not have a clue as to what to do, so he asked Savannah.

"You know Gina better than anyone else I know, besides her brother and sister-in-law, but I don't want to ask Glenda. I don't know, Savannah, I get the feeling that she really does not like Gina; that she only puts up with her because of Senator Ban."

"Glenda never had children so there may be a void in her life that has not been filled. That may explain the resentment," Savannah replied. "Do not be so hard on her, life without children to some women is painful."

"Senator Ban does not seem to want anyone in that family. He will not allow Mrs. Ban to see her family, and Gina said he told her that he had raised Gina and that was the only child he wanted. He really hates me, says that he does not want his sister to marry some dumbass jock; that his Gina is too good for that. It does not matter that I have a degree in Chemical Engineering and maintained a three point zero average in school."

"That is what I was afraid of," Savannah thought to herself, "that sick son of a bitch is in love with his own daughter. Somehow, I have got to get Gina away from him. But how? How am I going to do it?

"So, Gina and Ronny were engaged to be married when Gina killed herself, and that sick son of a bitch Ban was in love with Gina? But why did Gina kill herself; did she find out about you being her mother?"

"In time, Gemini; in time you will know it all, the whole story, now get out of here. Go home and get some rest." Savannah looked tired and she was about to hit the morphine pump again.

"DO YOU NOT REALIZE THE SERIOUSNESS OF THIS? YOUR ASS IS GOING TO SPEND THE REST OF YOUR LIFE IN THIS HOSPITAL IF YOU DO NOT TELL ME WHAT THE HELL HAPPENED!" I was screaming at her, partly out of frustration, partly out of fear; fear that I would not be able to save her.

My shouting made no difference to Savannah. She had already hit the morphine pump and was now in another world. I walked out of the room and down the hall to the elevator. I took the elevator down to the first floor, walked out of the hospital, across the street to the parking lot where I had left my car and got in. Then I locked the doors and cried like a baby.

I finally calmed myself down and drove back to the office. Antoinette was packing up for the day and as I was heading into the office, she informed me that Bookie had come by looking for me but, since I was not there, had decided to go home.

I entered my office without telling Antoinette good night, saw the motion that Ish had prepared and gave it a look over, although I knew how thorough he was, placed the motion in my briefcase, and left for the day. It would be an early night for me, Kyrra and I would curl up on the couch, eat popcorn, kettle was her favorite, and watch the news.

My dog was waiting for me when I walked through the door. I sat my case on the table in the dining room and made my way to my bedroom where I stripped down to my panties. I put on the doo-doo brown t-shirt with the two holes in the front and went into the kitchen to pop the corn. While the corn was popping in the microwave oven, I turned on the TV just in time to catch the early news. The story about the policemen arrested in the Shorty Hanes investigation was on, so I sat down next to my dog to watch it.

The footage showed the officers being escorted to the police station in handcuffs. I saw each one of them and as I watched each officer being taken out of a squad car, it made me wonder why they would do something so stupid and jeopardize their careers and the lives of their families.

Each officer held their head down, except for Ruth Loggins. She did not appear to be ashamed for her actions and I wondered how she could be so calm? She looked defiant as she looked into the cameras, almost as if she was having fun with all of this. Didn't she know that Omar Robinson was going to prosecute them to the fullest extent of the law, that they would probably spend two lifetimes in jail? If he could, Omar would let them die in prison, be buried, dug up, and placed back in prison to serve the full term. He was pissed, just like Bookie said, and the repercussions of what they did would affect the district attorney's office and the police department for months. Every dirt bag criminal and their lawyers would demand that their cases be reopened to see if there was evidence tampering involved in their case. And I was going to lead the way.

I watched the rest of the news, let Kyrra eat the rest of the popcorn, and headed for bed. Something about the news story was bothering me but I could not figure out what it was. Why would something so wonderful for my client bother me? But sleep was overtaking me and I was asleep before I could figure out why I had this feeling.

That same ill feeling stayed with me for the next few days as I entered the judge's chambers so that he could hear arguments on my motion to dismiss. My motion to dismiss the charges against my client was denied by the judge. Omar Robinson had provided a better argument for proceeding with the case and the judge agreed.

The next day I got a call from the DA's office, it was the great one himself, Omar Robinson. He wanted to meet with me ASAP and my gut feeling told me it would be something that I wanted to hear. I had Antoinette inform the partners that I would be meeting with Robinson and wanted to discuss it with them before I met with him.

I knew that Savannah would never make it to trial. Besides, I did not want it to come to that for a number of reasons. One, she was too sick to go through one; and two, I did not want to run the risk of her life and Gina's life being turned inside out. I did not want Savannah's memory to be tarnished by this whole affair. But as I was about to learn, sometimes the very thing that you think is wrong will turn out to be the right thing to do.

The meeting with the partners was not going to be a good one, at least that is how I saw it. I was going to tell them of my intentions of meeting with Robinson and taking a deal; a deal that my client could live with.

As I entered Quinn's office, I got the feeling that they had plans for me. I was right.

Basically, the meeting went like this: they wanted me to plea her out and be done with it. They had also received the report from her doctors and it would not be in Savannah's interest to go through a trial and I agreed. Besides, I was tired of fighting a battle she did not want me to fight.

I made plans to visit with her that morning after my talk with Omar. Then I was going to find Bookie, to tell him that I was sorry, and to try to make things right with him. We may not ever be anything more than what we were, friends, but that was better than not having him around at all.

I informed my staff about the decision and they agreed. The team had worked so hard on a possible defense for her, but they too had seen the report and knew that there was no use fighting this in court. Let Savannah live out what little time she had left in the hospital; I was sure that Robinson would agree to that.

My meeting with him took place a few hours later in his office.

"Gemini, I think you know why you are here." He looked so smug that I almost said that I wanted to continue the fight, I hated losing to him. But once I thought about it, I wasn't losing; I was just doing what was best for my client, for my friend.

"Yes, Omar, I know why I am here. I have spoken with the partners and they want me to plea this one out. So, she stays in the hospital for the time that she has left, which isn't long."

"Yes."

"Agreed."

"Well, I guess that is it then, I want to thank you for your time and I hope to do battle with you again real soon. I hear that your office is going to represent some of the officers accused of working for Shorty Hanes. More than likely you will be assigned the case."

"I do not think so, they would have mentioned it to me already, and they may be giving Jason Wheeler another shot to redeem himself."

"Damn, I was hoping it would be you. I love doing battle with worthy opponents."

"Well, Omar Robinson, I am surprised that you would consider me a worthy opponent. I don't know whether to be flattered or cautious, or both."

"Oh make no mistake about it, Gemini, I do consider you a worthy opponent, and I do not make that statement lightly. I know the real Gemini, the woman behind the warrior spirit and the commanding presence."

"Now you make me sound like a member of SWAT. Is that how I come across to you?"

"On the contrary, Gemini. You come across as a force to be reckoned with."

We resumed our talk about the case. "The hearing for Ms. Wooten will take place in few days after I inform the judge that an agreement has been reached by us. Then you can concentrate on your client's health and this should also satisfy the people I serve, as well as Ban's widow."

"Does she know about Savannah's condition?"

"My office informed her, yes."

"Did you inform her about your theory of the affair?"

"She was the one who gave the police the information about the affair."

I was up and out of the office and headed for my car before Omar Robinson figured out I was gone.

If Glenda Ban suspected an affair, why did she invite Savannah to the press conference? What the hell was she up to and why? There were only two people who could answer these questions and I was going to talk to both of them. One was dying and the other was supposedly grieving, but I had a hunch they were both laughing.

I was going to see Glenda Ban first, and I was going unannounced. I needed some answers and I needed them now, not for my client because if I was right, Savannah knew all of the answers, but I needed to know for myself to put all of the pieces of this puzzle together.

I reached the Bans and was surprised when Glenda answered the door. It was obvious that she was waiting for someone else to arrive because of the look of surprise on her face.

"Ms. Jones, I was not expecting you. I wished you had called before you came over, I would have told you that I would have to meet with you at another time."

"Or it would have given you time to call your brother to come over and be with you and help you stay out of jail."

"What do you mean, out of jail? I have done nothing wrong. It was my husband that was murdered, remember; by your client."

"Yes, and it was you who invited my client to the press conference. That is what I want to talk to you about. Why did you invite her to the press conference?"

"Why not invite her? After all, she is well known in the community and we have worked on some charities together. Besides, she was very fond of Gina and I thought it was something that Gina would have done."

I knew that I was not going to get the truth from her; she was lying and I knew it. I just couldn't figure out what she was lying about, or why. I decided to get the truth from Savannah; after all, she owed me that much. Glenda Ban was going to cover her ass till the end, but that was not going to stop me from pressing her further.

"Did you tell the police that you suspected my client was having an affair with your husband? Do you know the truth, Mrs. Ban; do you know the history between my client and your husband?"

"All I know is that my husband is burning in hell right now and your client put him there."

"I think she had some help putting him there from you."

"And I think, no, I know, it is time for you to leave." She stood up and I knew it was my cue to leave also, but not before I gave her something to think about.

"I will not stop until I get the truth. Please do not think for one moment that this is over, because believe me, it is not."

I was walking to the door when Glenda replied, "Maybe you should talk with Savannah before you decide."

"I intend to, Mrs. Ban. I intend to."

When I arrived at the hospital, I was told by the nurse on duty that they had been trying to reach my office, Savannah wanted to see me. As I entered Savannah's room, I saw a woman sitting in one of the chairs and I knew in an instant who she was. It was Mrs. Gill, Savannah's mother. She looked up at me and got up for me to take the chair. I motioned for her to remain seated, she sat back down and it looked as if it took every ounce of her strength to do so. Savannah was asleep, I could hear her gently snoring so I pulled up a chair to talk with Mrs. Gill.

"You must be Gemini, my daughter has spoken of you often through the years; she calls you her cussing angel. I want to thank you for all that you have done and did for her."

"You are welcome, Mrs. Gill; I turned to look at Savannah, how is she doing?"

The doctor was in here today to examine her. He said he is giving her two months at the most." She started to cry. "My baby has given up on life, and there is nothing that I can do about it. It isn't natural for a parent to outlive their child, I feel so helpless. I look to God for answers, and he's being very silent on this one."

"Momma, God is being silent because you already know the answer, it is my time and I am ready to go." Savannah was sitting up now, despite her appearance. The cancer had travelled quickly. She was as thin as a rail and had a gaunt look in her face, but her voice was strong and I got the feeling that she wanted to talk with me, to tell me something, which is why she had had the nurse call me.

"Momma, I want to talk with Gemini for a while. Is Poppa downstairs? If so, why don't you leave now and you can come back tomorrow to see me, okay?"

"Okay, baby girl," Mrs. Gill replied. "Your daddy been downstairs all the time, I keep trying to get him to come up but you know your daddy."

"His only child is dying and he can't come and see about her?" It came out of my mouth before I knew it.

Mrs. Gill turned to me and said, "Ms. Gemini, please don't judge my husband too badly. He has always been a hard man, just like his daddy was, and he don't know what to do to change. He's been so mad for so long, somebody got to show him how to make things right, I just don't know what I can say to help him. He's mad at himself, mad that he couldn't protect his little girl, and every time he looks at her, it reminds him of how he failed to protect her from that demon David Ban. Maybe you can say something to him, it isn't right that his only child is dying and he won't come up to see her."

"Let me speak to Savannah first, and then tomorrow, I will make it a point to stop by and see you and Elder Gill."

"That will be fine." She wrote down the address and handed it to me.

"I won't say anything to him; I'll just let him be surprised." She left the room and went to her husband.

"Gemini, you do not have to go over there and try to talk some sense into my daddy. Once he gets something in his head, no one can get reason with him."

"A trait that you seemed to have inherited from him," I replied, and sat in the chair next to the bed.

"We need to talk, Savannah. First of all, the DA and I have come up with an agreement that I think you will be happy with. You will plead guilty to man one and serve the remaining time in the hospital; you will pay for the entire stay here. Is that something that you can live with?"

"No pun intended, Gemini?" Savannah laughed. "Is that something I can live with; I guess so, since I don't have to live with it long."

"None of this shit is funny. You have been holding out a lot on me, and now I want to know the whole truth. From the beginning, I want to know what went on. Why did Gina kill herself, and what does Glenda Ban have to do with all of this?"

"If I tell you the whole story, promise me that you will not use any of this against Glenda. That woman suffered enough with what David put her through."

"How can you defend the woman? She told the police that you were having an affair with her husband."

"She told the police what I told her to tell them."

"Why the hell did you do that?"

"To protect the memory of my daughter. I did all of this for Gina."

Chapter 14

One year and three months before David Ban
went to his ancestors.

Ban was sitting at his desk in the new home he had built for himself and Gina; he had not cared if Glenda moved in or not. He was wondering how the hell that bitch Savannah had become a part of Gina's life and how in the name of God had he allowed Gina to become engaged to Ronny Washington. He had been so busy with the upcoming announcement of his running for governor, that he had not spent a lot of time with her. Now she was engaged to that damn football player Washington and that bitch of a mother of her's was being photographed in the papers with her.

The local paper had run the story about Gina and Ronny's engagement, and the fact that her friend, Savannah Wooten, founder and owner of Highly Favored, had helped to plan the proposal and the engagement party. Washington had arranged for the two of them to go to the movies and with the help of the manager, he had paid for the proposal to appear on the screen when the previews were showing.

The bitch had wanted to help with the cost of the damn party, but that had come out of his pocket, Glenda had seen to that. She hadn't bothered to tell him jack shit. The Ghost thought the engagement had come at a good time and had instructed Ban that he would be happy about it in the press, whether he liked it or not. The nine-carat diamond engagement ring she had on her finger only made Ban even madder. Mad because he wanted to buy her rings like that. He wanted to be the only man to give her gifts like that. After all, she was his true love and he was waiting for the time to tell her how he felt. She would be a little *sickened by it at first, but in time, she would understand how much he loved her and would come to his way of thinking.*

But first, there were two people that he had to get rid of, Ronny Washington and that bitch Savannah.

Gina was still in bed and had told the staff that she was sleeping in. The party had lasted well into the morning with the last guest leaving about five a.m. That bitch Savannah had come, he still could not believe that she had become friends with his Gina and not bothered to tell her the truth. But Gina would never know the truth, she would never know who the bitch really was; he would see to that.

The last time he had seen Savannah was shortly before his father gave him the ultimatum, jail or the army. Two weeks ago he saw her for the first time in years and the hatred that he felt for her was just as strong as the day he enlisted in the army. Gina had brought her by the house to meet him. She had been telling him about her friend Savannah, but he really did not make the connection. Until he saw her, then he knew.

As they walked into his study that fateful day two weeks earlier, he was preparing to sit Gina down and tell her why he did not approve of Washington. When he looked up and saw Savannah, thoughts of Washington quickly left his head; he had an even bigger problem.

"David, I want you meet my friend and mentor, Savannah Wooten. She is the founder and owner of Highly Favored, that agency that I have been working with. The community center and Highly Favored are doing a lot of projects together. In the spring, we plan to start several community gardens in the city to sell the produce in the fall and to teach young people how to garden. You and Savannah have made all this possible." She turned to Savannah and said, "My brother founded the community center and was instrumental in a lot of services being set up here for the citizens. He has done a lot for the people in this area."

"I have heard so many good things about you, Mr. Ban. Your sister talks about you all the time. She is very proud of you. Now she has two good men in her life, you and Ronny." If what she suspected was true, he did not like the remark that she had just made, and the sudden flash of anger she saw in his eyes told her she was right.

Life had been kind to his appearance. He took very good care of himself. It was known in Kingsford Heights that he always thought that he looked like a black Paul Newman; and she could still see it in his face. But the eyes, his eyes always had that faraway look in them, just as they had when he was younger. There was no life in them, no soul. That is what it was; David Ban looked as if he never had a soul.

"That bitch looks the same," Ban thought. Like him, life had been very good to Savannah. She now wore her hair past her shoulders and had dyed it golden bronze, which suited her skin color. She was still model thin but had the butt in the back that black

woman are famous for. He had to admit that she was wearing those jeans well and for a brief moment, he wished things had been different. But now she was taunting him, with the remark that she made about him and Washington being in Gina's life.

He had to come up with an excuse to get Gina out of the room so he could set this bitch straight. Just who in the hell does she think she is coming here after all these years to lay claim on his daughter? Did she think that she had a chance to be Gina's mother? The only mother Gina knew was dead and as far as he was concerned, Gina would go to her grave believing that. No way was Savannah or anyone else going to tell Gina the truth. He had to protect her and his reputation at all cost.

"Gina, I have a new jazz cassette tape I meant to bring down here to listen to. Will you go upstairs and look for it for me. Selma will help you look, she is upstairs now. Do that for big brother, will you?" There was no cassette, but knowing Gina and how much she liked doing things for him, he knew she would be up there for quite some time. Then he would have his "talk" with Savannah. He would get that bitch out of their lives for good.

Once Gina was gone, her parents faced each other for the first time since David was forced from his home and into the Army.

"Just what the hell do you call yourself doing," David spat the words out with the hatred clinging to each one. "Get the hell out of here while you can."

"I'm not glad to see you either, but for Gina's sake, I will fake it. And know this, I have no intention of getting out of her life, not now or ever, and there is nothing you or anyone else can do about it."

"And I suppose that you intend to tell her who you really are. Well, I would not if I were you."

"You may think that I am the same little girl that you raped years ago, but I am not. And when I tell you that I am not afraid of you, believe me, I am not."

"You should be, bitch; you should be."

"And you should be just as afraid of me. I for one know what a sick bastard you really are. I was only eleven, remember?"

"Not really, you weren't that good."

"Did you really expect an eleven-year- old to be? You really are a sick son of a bitch in love with his own daughter." The look in his eyes was a mixture of hatred and fear, and it gave her the courage to continue.

"You are not going to ruin her life, and if you think that I am going to let you, you got another thing coming. I love that girl and I will protect her with my life. But I really don't think you are going to do anything to stop this friendship; you're scared, scared that I am going to tell Gina the truth, but I won't. I won't hurt her like that. She thinks that *you are her brother and despite being the sick bastard that you are, you have managed to raise her well. I have to thank you and Glenda for that."*

"My wife had nothing to do with how Gina turned out; she hates her with a passion."

"She hates the fact that you refused to have children with her, which is the best idea you have come up with. She just doesn't know how big a favor you did for her."

"I did you a favor a few years ago; on your way to school."

"You think taking advantage of me and raping me was doing me a favor? You really are sick."

"May I remind you that my family and staff are around and can easily walk in on this discussion?"

"I don't mind shouting it from your roof. I want the whole world to know how big a devil you really are, I just won't because of Gina."

"You should be concerned for your own life, not just Gina's."

"Are you threatening me? Because if you are, like the young folk say, bring it on. Let's tell the whole state about their golden boy, who thinks he bears a slight resemblance to Paul Newman; Paul Newman with no soul."

That remark sent Ban over the edge, Savannah liked the fact that she could get a reaction out of him.

"YOU DO NOT KNOW WHO YOU ARE MESSING WITH, SAVANNAH GILL. BELIEVE ME, YOU DON'T KNOW AND YOU DON'T WANT TO KNOW. I WOULD SUGGEST THAT YOU LEAVE HERE NOW AND LEAVE GINA ALONE!"

"How dare you talk to my friend like that. What is wrong with you?" It was Gina returning from the little errand he'd sent her on. "Savannah is my friend, and my guest, and if you have a problem with that, then it's your problem!"

Savannah reacted before Ban could recover. "Gina, your brother is just worried that I may be occupying too much of your time; he just wants to make sure that you stay focused on your studies and on your upcoming wedding to Ronny." She knew that last remark made Ban mad as hell.

"That does not excuse what he just said to you." She turned to David. "I know that you still think of me as your little sister, but I am not. I am grown, in college, and about to marry the man of my dreams."

Savannah saw Ban flinch when Gina made the last statement. "He is going to stop this marriage from taking place; I feel it, so I have got to stay close to Gina to keep it from happening," she thought.

"And I am sure that your brother respects the fact that you are making good decisions concerning your future. It is just that he is under a lot of pressure right now, wouldn't you say so, David? May I call you David?"

"Nice touch, bitch," Ban thought, then turned to his daughter. "Gina, I am sorry about the outburst, I have been under a lot of pressure lately; and you are right, you are grown and making some good decisions. Forgive me, dearest Gina."

"Only if you promise me the biggest wedding ever, dearest David. Then and only then will I forgive you."

Gina walked over to her brother and gave him a hug and a kiss. Savannah watched and was sickened by the look on Ban's face. He looked like a love-struck schoolboy and that made Savannah sick to her stomach. There was a movement on her right that made Savannah turn in that direction. She saw Glenda Ban observing the same scene and the look on her face bothered Savannah even more than David's. It was the look of madness, pure evil, and unbridled hatred. She knew then that somehow she was going to have to get Gina out of this house. Gina's sanity and her life depended on it.

"So, Glenda hated Gina and her husband. Is that what you're telling me, Savannah?"

"She hated both of them with a passion. She hated Gina because of David's love for her and David for not wanting children with her. I felt sorry for her, but I was afraid for Gina at the same time."

"Then why do you want to protect her? She hated your daughter."

"I am not protecting Glenda, I am protecting Gina. I do not want her memory soiled any more than it is. After all, she committed suicide and the press had a field day with her death, all because of David and his sick obsession with her. She shot herself, Gemini, and she died alone, thinking the worst about herself and David. And most of what she was told was a lie." The tears were flowing down Savannah's face now and the conversation had taken its toll on her.

"I'm tired, my cussing angel. Now, go home and try not to think about this. Whatever Robinson offers you, take it. I am not going to fight this, as I have told you before."

"I have to stop by your parents' first. There are a few things that I want to say to your father, things that should have been said to him a long time ago."

"You heard my momma, Gemini. He's an old man and forgiveness is hard for him."

"He's an old man who needs to let go of the past and live out his life grudge free. I am going just as your mother requested, and this time, I am not taking any orders from you."

I got up and left before Savannah could respond.

The Gills' home was close to the hospital, and when I arrived, Mrs. Gill let me in. Elder Gill was in his living room, reading the Bible, and looked up as Mrs. Gill and I walked in. Mrs. Gill made the introductions.

"Earl, this is Savannah's lawyer, Gemini Jones."

Elder Gill did not say anything, he just stared at me. I decided to speak.

"Elder Gill, I am here on behalf of your daughter. She is very ill and needs all the support she can get. Her prognosis is not good, and it would be nice if she had all those who love her around her at this time. I am fighting for her and I need for you and your wife to do the same."

That statement got a response. "You are the person who cursed me when my wife, mother, and I came to get Savannah after her disgrace."

"Disgrace! Disgrace? You call being raped at eleven by a grown-ass man a disgrace? She was only a child, an innocent child, and there was no one to protect her when David Ban raped her! How can you sit there after all these years and blame your daughter for what David Ban did? What kind of God do you serve?" I knew I had made a mistake with that remark but I could never control my anger.

Elder Gill was livid. As he stood up, the Bible that he was reading fell to the floor. Before he could reach down for it, I reached down and picked it up and held it in my hands as I continued giving him a piece of my mind.

"You can't forgive yourself, can you? That is what has been eating at you all these years. You can't forgive yourself for not being able to prevent what happened to your daughter. After I left Mamie Wells's home and returned to my own, my father couldn't look me in the eye or talk with me for weeks."

"I am not your father, young lady, and you have no right to talk to a man of God like this."

"A man of God who has blamed his daughter for something that she had no control over."

"She murdered a man, took a life; what do you call that?" By this time he was in my face and I could feel little drops of spittle on my face.

"She murdered a monster as far as I am concerned, a man that raped her; that fathered her child, raised that child as his own, and then was responsible for that child's death." He was startled by my remark.

"Yes, Elder Gill, David Ban was responsible for the death of your grandchild, your only grandchild."

That remark made Mrs. Gill gasp, it was as if she were hearing this for the first time. "His wife never said that, she said that Gina killed herself."

"His wife? What do you mean his wife? Have you been talking to her?" I was asking Mrs. Gill.

"Yes, she seemed very interested in Savannah and Gina."

"Interested in what way?"

I noticed the guilty look in Mrs. Gill's eyes and I knew that she had something that she was hiding from me, and more importantly, from Savannah.

"Did she ask you about Savannah being Gina's mother?" I knew that I had hit the nail on the head; that was exactly what Glenda Ban had done.

"She did mention that Savannah and Gina favored and wondered if we could be related to her. She said that Gina didn't know very much about her parents since they were killed when she was young. Did you know that David never told Gina anything about her parents and Gina tried several times to get him to talk about them but he wouldn't? So she thought that since we lived in the same town and David and his family that we could give her some information about Gina's parents."

"Did you tell her that Savannah was Gina's mother? Your answer can mean a great deal to this case if you did."

"Gemini, she already knew, she told me she did." The fear in her eyes made me stop dead in my tracks; she thought that I was going to tell Savannah about her conversation with Glenda. And she was right, I was.

"Did you tell Savannah about this? Did she know that Glenda knew?"

"Yes, I told her the day after Mrs. Ban called when I met her for lunch. I told her that Glenda Ban knew and that she felt that it was only right that Gina know too. Savannah was so upset with me and with Glenda that she did not even finish her lunch, she just ran out of the restaurant and drove off."

"How long ago was that? You have got to remember, Mrs. Gill. How long ago did you tell Savannah about your conversation with Glenda?"

"About a week before Gina killed herself." That statement made her start to cry. Elder Gill heard the conversation and seemed visibly upset.

"It's sin; that's what it is, sin! That demon Ban raped my baby and ruined her life and her baby's life. I should have killed that evil son of a bitch when this first happened; I should have sent him straight to hell!" He started to cry and his wife went to him and hugged him. I knew two things: one, he was finally coming to terms with the past. And two, it was time for me to leave.

I went back to the office, called Omar Robinson, and told him that Savannah had agreed to the deal. He then told me that his office would inform me of the court date and that it would be held at the hospital, since Savannah was too ill to come to court. She would have to explain her actions for the record and then the judge would impose the sentence. He was also holding a press conference this afternoon to inform the public about the decision. This would satisfy the Ban family; and the citizens, who seemed to love Ban and wanted his murderer punished. I was the only one who was pissed; the only one who was not satisfied. I wanted to find out how much Glenda Ban was involved in this and I wanted her punished also. I had a feeling that she had a lot more to do with this whole affair than she was letting on. I believed that she knew more about this than even Savannah thought that she did. And I was going to find out. I knew that I was going to have to speak to Ronny Washington. He could tie some of this together for me; I felt it in my guts. I was going to have to get in touch with him, and fast. I needed to know the truth, and I needed to know now.

I got home and was met at the door by Kyrra, who wanted to go outside and take care of her business. I let her out in the backyard and turned on the television in time to catch the evening news.

The reporter was telling the story of the police officers who had tampered with evidence and that they had started to turn on each other, all of them blaming each other as being the ringleader. The only one who, according to the news story, was remaining silent was Ruth Loggins; she was refusing to give a statement to the police about her role in this crime. I watched the old footage of the police being taken to court for their arraignment and again I was struck by Ruth Loggins's demeanor. She looked straight into the camera, as if she wanted the world to know who she was and what she had done. Kyrra's hitting the back door to be let in made me forget that story and after a while, I started to prepare myself some dinner.

I checked my phone messages and saw that Bookie had called and left a message for me to call him back. I was so glad that I forgot I was cooking spaghetti and only remembered when I heard the water spilling over the pot and onto the stove.

I dialed his number and he answered on the second ring. I was nervous, but I tried to remain calm. After all, I was talking with a friend and colleague, what did I have to be scared about? He knew I was nervous the minute I opened my mouth.

"You called?"

"Yes, all my Gemini, I did. What are you so nervous about; you got something you want to say to me?" That remark made me mad. Damn, he was the one who called, not me.

"You called me, that tells me that you have something that you want to say to me." I was pissed and he knew it.

"All my Gemini, I just wanted to say that I hope you did not think that I was upset with you for the other day. I know you too damn well to take anything you say and get upset behind it. But I do want to talk with you about something, only I think it needs to be done face to face. So, I want to come over now and talk, I'll bring dinner if you want."

"I am cooking spaghetti for one, but I could stretch it if I have to."

"I'll bring the wine. Just so you know, I had to go to Indianapolis for the firm. The partners are thinking about representing some reality TV show star and wanted me to check them out before they make their decision. You know my Uncle Quinn, he is very selective about who the firm represents. I have had time to think about a lot while I was down there and it had to do with you. See you in a few minutes."

We both said good-bye and hung up. I sat down on the couch because, by now, my knees were shaking so badly. What in the hell did he want with me? I know that there is some chemistry between us, was he going to try to act on those feelings? And if so, was I going to act on my feelings for him as well? My imagination ran away with me and I decided to put my imagination on hold and wait for the talk. I have been guilty of letting my imagination run wild in the past, and it has always gotten my feelings hurt and my heart broken. You would think that by now I would have learned my lesson.

He arrived about twenty minutes later carrying a bottle of wine and looking like he was posing for GQ magazine. His leather jacket had to have set him back a couple of thousand dollars and I knew the jeans were at least $300 by themselves. His green shirt was silk and he had a leather cap to match the jacket. I knew I was looking at $3000 dollars' worth of clothing. Boy did he wear it well! He stood in the doorway for a moment, savoring the moment I told myself, and then said one of his crazy statements just to break the silence.

"Why are you looking at me like I just stepped off of a spaceship? Are you going to let me in or what?" He did not wait for me to answer but simply walked past me and set the wine on the dinner table. " I closed the door, but remained silent. "Did the cat get your tongue while I was on my way over? What's up girlfriend, talk to Bookie Lyman."

"Why in the hell didn't you let me know where you were going? You were supposed to be working on Savannah's case with me and you just up and leave without letting me know!"

"I'm glad to see you too, "he replied. "I was working for the people who pay my salary. You know them, they pay your six figure salary too!"

"Why are you here, Bookie? What is this revelation that you had while you were away on assignment!"

"We have plenty of time to get to that, now tell me what is going on with Savannah."

I did what I was told, while I finished dinner. Bookie set the table and poured the wine. I told him about the deal that I had made with Robinson and that the partners had agreed. I told him about the conversations I had with Savannah's parents and Glenda Ban. I also told him that I needed to talk with Ronny Washington because I felt that he held the key to a lot of this. Bookie agreed. He said that he would arrange for me to meet with Washington. He told me that his people were very protective of him right now since Gina's death, but that he could arrange for us to meet.

The moment of our talk finally came after dinner—which was very good, I must say for myself, and Bookie agreed. My heart was racing as fast as my imagination and I tried to slow them down, but to no avail.

"Gemini, I had a lot of time to think while I was away and a lot of what I had to think about was you and me. You must know that I have feelings for you, and you don't have to be a rocket scientist to figure out that you feel the same way. That is why you got so upset when you thought that I was spending time with my ex."

"And you want to discuss what we are going to do about it, is that it?"

"No, Gemini, I know what I want to do; I just want to know if you want the same thing? I know you have a problem with the age difference. After all, you don't want to be known as a cougar." He knew me so well. "But that should not, and does not, matter. What matters is if we do decide to take this to another level and it does not work out, what happens to our friendship?"

"I would think that we wouldn't be friends anymore and would make it difficult to work together. I care for you, Bookie, I have to admit. But I care about your friendship more, and I care that we have a great working relationship. I don't want that to be jeopardized."

He looked at me and I melted on the inside. I really did want this, but I knew that doing so could ruin what we already had. And I really wanted Bookie to, above all else, be my friend.

"So that's it then, we remain as we are; good friends to the end?" It sounded so final coming from him, we both knew that we was right.

We finished the evening laughing and talking as Bookie told me about his trip to Indy. The firm was going to represent a reality show star, Marquise Crawford, in a lawsuit with the show's producers.

He had me laughing about how outrageous she was and the name of the show was a hoot. The show was called "Make Me Beautiful" and the hostess was nicknamed "the Beast." I thought that was awful and told Bookie that. He laughed because part of the high ratings of the show was because viewers, for the most part, thought Marquise was very unattractive and wanted her to get plastic surgery, which she refused to do and that kept the ratings high.

Bookie left just in time for me to catch the nightly news. They were talking about the evidence scandal and the stepfather of Ruth Loggins was talking to the press about his stepdaughter. He spoke about how he and his wife were sticking behind their daughter, and that in America, you were innocent until proven guilty. I turned off the TV still thinking about the story and the fact that one of those policemen had done my client a favor.

It was three in the morning when I sat up and realized who had gotten rid of the gun for Savannah and why. She had aged of course, and had gained weight over the years, but the eyes, they had that same defiant look. It was the little girl that shared the same hell as Savannah and I during the summer of 1971. She too had gotten pregnant and had ended up in Bitch Wells's home. It was Ruthie, little Ruthie Summers. I didn't know whether to laugh or cry. I ended up doing both.

Chapter 15

Hell on Earth; Home of Mamie Wells

There had been several weeks of peace between Gemini, Mamie, and Savannah, and it looked as if the three had finally come to some sort of truce. Mamie had not bothered Savannah in a while but had started in on another girl who looked like Savannah, Ruthann Summers. Ruthann was fourteen years old, pregnant by her stepfather, and a mental mess. Her parents were Catholic so there was no way she could have an abortion. The child would be adopted so that Ruthann could come home and continue to live her life. She had not told her mother what her stepfather had done, mainly out of fear, but had confided in Savannah and Gemini. Her stepfather held a high position in the police department and she knew what he was capable of.

Mamie constantly tormented Ruthann about being pregnant and not knowing whom to name as the father. She made fun of her in front of all the other girls and even Lucy and Cora asked her to stop. But Bitch Wells was enjoying herself, and making life miserable for Ruthann made her forget how miserable she really was.

The day that Gemini almost beat Mamie Wells to death started off like any other day, except that Ruthann had gone into labor. The doctor was out of town so it looked as if Mamie would be the one to help with the delivery.

Savannah and Gemini could hear Ruthann shouting in her room across the hall from theirs and decided to go in to help.

Ruthann looked as if death was at her door. She was pale and the sweat was pouring out of her like a waterfall. Her dress and bed were soaked with her sweat and she yelled to the top of her voice when they entered the room.

"*Gemini, we have got to help her,*" *Savannah said.* "*She is in a lot of pain, run and tell Miss Wells so that she can come a help her!*"

"*Bitch Wells knows she's like this, she is making her suffer 'cause she's a sick bitch. Well, I am going to get her and make her help. You stay here with Ruthann till I come back.*"

Savannah agreed and went over to the bed to comfort Ruthann while Gemini went to look for Wells. She held Ruthann in her little arms as Ruthann moaned and groaned in pain. She even said a prayer for Ruthann, for herself and Gemini, and for their unborn babies. She even prayed for Bitch Wells and her mother, father, and Nana.

Gemini found Bitch Wells in the kitchen chatting with Cora and Lucy. She was sitting at the table sipping tea like it was Sunday morning brunch. She did not notice Gemini had entered the room but the look on Lucy and Cora's faces told her that someone else was in the room.

"*Ruthann is in labor, ain't you gonna help her get to the nursery so that she can have her baby?*" *Gemini said.*

"*That ain't none of your business how I handle my home. You need to go back to your room and stay out of grown folk business.*"

Gemini was walking toward Mamie now and was determine to pursue the subject.

"*You gotta stop sitting here like you the Queen of England; get upstairs and help Ruthann, she is about to have her baby.*"

"*And I told you to stay out of grown folk business,*" *Mamie stood up and faced Gemini with a false sense of courage, she was scared to death and Gemini knew it.*

"*You ain't nothing but a cold hearted bitch and I will kick your ass if you don't get Ruthann some help, and I mean now.*"

Mamie did not get a chance to respond, the first punch hit her dead in the middle of her stomach which sent Mamie to the floor. Then came the kicking which seemed to come from different directions and hit every major part of her body, her head, face, back, legs, arms, you name the part of the body; it got hit. And the pain was so bad that it made Mamie cry out for Gemini to stop, she pleaded with Gemini to stop.

Cora and Lucy tried to grab Gemini, but both of them were no match for her. They decided it would be best for them to look after Ruthann and they both left the room running.

By the time Gemini stopped kicking Mamie, there was blood all over the floor, all Mamie's of course. She managed to crawl to a chair and sit in it, but the pain in her side made her bend over and she hit the floor again.

"*You are going to pay for this, you crazy bitch,*" *Mamie hissed at Gemini.* "*I will have the last laugh, crazy bitch.*"

"You can have the last laugh, after you get your black ass in there and help Ruthann, "Gemini spat back and left the room.

But Mamie, in no condition to help herself let alone Ruthann, just sat there.

"I don't give a damn if you have to crawl up those stairs, if you don't get your black, hateful ass upstairs and take care of that girl and her baby, I am going to kill you. And you know that I am crazy enough to do that."

"What about your own baby? You're so busy fighting me that you could be doing damage to your own baby. You want it to come out deformed, or crazy like you?" Mamie thought that would put some sense in the crazy bitch's head. She was wrong.

Gemini reached down, grabbed Mamie by her hair, and started dragging her across the floor. When they reached the foot of the stairs, Gemini let her go and Mamie went flying up the stairs, the pain hitting her with each step. But it was better than staying where she was, she didn't know what that crazy bitch was going to do next.

By the time they both reached Ruthann's room, she was screaming at the top of her lungs. Savannah was at her side and holding on to her, wiping her brow, and silently praying. Cora and Lucy were no help; they just stood there and waited for Mamie to give orders.

It was too late to call the doctor, so Mamie had to act as the midwife. She ordered Gemini and Savannah to leave the room, but neither one of them would, so she continued assisting Ruthann with the delivery.

Ruthann delivered a healthy baby boy. She didn't want to see the baby at first, but Savannah convinced her to see him, she told Ruthie that not seeing him would come back to haunt her. She would always wonder what he looked like. Ruthann asked to have the baby spend the night with her and Mamie, out of fear, broke her own rule and allowed it. Savannah and Gemini stayed with Ruthann that night and helped her with the baby. Ruthann was the older than Savannah, but that night she felt like the baby with Savannah playing the role of her mother. Savannah seemed to know what to do and comfort her and she was grateful.

Even Gemini was amazed at how Savannah seemed to forget her problems and concentrate on Ruthann, offering her comfort and helping her with the baby. She even sang a song to help put the baby to sleep and the song soothed Ruthann and Gemini. She had a nice voice that didn't quite hit every note but the tone was soothing and you could feel the warmth and the love. For that one night, the three of them were comforted being together; their hell didn't seem so bad that night.

The next day the baby was placed in the nursery and Ruthann had to say good-bye to her son. She would not be allowed to see him after today. Gemini was on high alert; she was anticipating there being some trouble with Mamie, especially if Ruthann wanted to see the baby again and Mamie wouldn't allow it. But when it was time to give up the *baby, Ruthann did fine, she was ready to let go. Savannah stayed with her another day and finally went back to her room to rest and be with Gemini.*

The baby was adopted two days later. Ruthann was not allowed to watch the baby leave, but Savannah stayed with her while Gemini snuck into the attic and watched the departure from the window. She would see as much as she could so that she would be able to tell Ruthann when she was ready to hear it. But for now, it was her and Savannah's secret.

Ruthann's family came the next day to take Ruthann home. It was too much for Ruthann to take, the thought of going home to be in the same house as him. She cried and held on to Savannah until Lucy came up to tell her that her parents were downstairs waiting to take her home. It was Savannah who got her to get herself together and walk downstairs. It was Savannah who stood at the head of the stairs and watched Ruthann as she walked down to meet her parents. It was Savannah's strength that willed her down those stairs and she would never forget the little girl whose heart was as big as her belly!

I finally stopped crying about an hour before I was to get up and start the day. When I thought about what Ruthann had done, how she had become a bad cop to hurt her stepfather and how she had disposed of the gun that killed David Ban for Savannah, I wanted to cry more. Partly out of gratitude and partly out of fear, fear that I would have to go to the police and tell them. After all, I was an officer of the court and sworn to uphold the law, but how could I do this without everything coming out about Savannah, Ban, and Gina. It would kill Savannah if the story got out; and I could not afford that. And the political scandal would be horrific!

I would schedule a meeting with Quinn when I got to work and talk it over with him. If I did not have to say anything, I wouldn't. But if I had to report what I knew to the police, I would have to have time to prepare for the shit to hit the fan. All of our lives would be exposed and how would the firm fare through this. Damn, life was hard!

It was no use trying to lie in bed until the alarm went off since I was already awake, so I got up and got ready. I fed myself, Kyrra, and my plants and left before the sun was up. I got to work before Antoinette, so I made the coffee, which I mixed with coco and waited for Quinn to arrive.

Quinn arrives at work before most of the people in the office, including his secretary. I could run in and see him before his secretary arrived and I could have an informal chat about what I thought.

Quinn arrived about ten minutes after I did and I caught him in the hall. He was surprised to see me.

"Gemini, I usually don't see you this early. Is something wrong with the way the case is going?"

"I'm not sure," I replied "That is what I wanted to talk to you about."

He invited me in and I told him the story and my theory.

"You want to know if this is something that you have to go to the police with, is that it?"

"Yes. Am I obligated to go to the police?"

"Do you know that this officer was the one that got rid of the gun?"

"No, but I would bet my year's salary she did."

"But you have no proof?"

"No."

"And would this be in the best interest of your client; haven't you reached an agreement with Robinson?"

"Yes, and he will be holding the press conference today to announce the deal." Then the thought accorded to me. "He may be hard to reach today, being so busy getting ready for the press conference. And today is Friday, so if I can't get in touch with him today, I would have to wait until Monday," I said.

"Then we will wait and talk about it Monday." That statement shocked the hell out of me, wait till Monday? That did not sound like Quinn; he liked to be well ahead of the game. But I would do exactly what he wanted me to do; I would wait until Monday.

I would, however, tell Savannah today. I would also check with Bookie to see if he had gotten in touch with Ronny Washington. I wanted to know Glenda Ban's role in all of this and I was like a dog with a bone.

Antoinette was shocked when she got to work and found me there and the coffee made. I asked to her let me know when Bookie came in and then I just sat with my head leaned back in my chair and rested my eyes. I was dog tired and remembered that I had not bothered to take my medicine that morning, but I would do it at lunchtime.

Bookie came an hour later to tell me that he had arranged for me to meet with Washington. On Monday, he would be in town. He was looking forward to talking with me and I was looking forward to talking with him. He told Bookie that he was concerned about Savannah and told Bookie that if she needed anything, help with the hospital bill or anything, just let him know. I was touched by that and would make sure that I tell her when I went to visit her today.

I told Bookie about my meeting with Quinn. I told him about Ruthann and what I thought about her disposing of the gun that killed Ban. He did not seem to be that upset and told me so.

"Gemini, what is the big ass deal? I mean, the DA has all the evidence they need to convict them. Their theory is backed by cold, hard evidence that the cops got sloppy and destroyed evidence they did not have to destroy. It has not even occurred to them that the missing gun is nothing more than that. So let them think just that; all they want is a conviction and that is what they are going to get."

"I hope that you are right, Bookie. But Quinn did say to wait until Monday, so I will wait until Monday."

"And I say wait until the Monday after hell freezes over, all my Gemini. Let it go; if you think something bad is going to happen, it will; so let it go."

Bookie didn't know how right he was.

Monday came and went and still I did not go to the police with what I knew. Quinn did not say anything to me about what we had discussed so I did not mention it either. I visited with Savannah, she was upset over an incident that had occurred in her room earlier, and I spent the better portion of my visit with her trying to understand just what had happened. Members of the press had gotten into her room, I talked with the guard who had been placed outside her room from the beginning. The hospital staff was upset by the whole affair, and the manager of oncology and the head of security assured me that it would not happened again.

Over the past few weeks after the murder, Savannah had been crucified by the press. After all, she was being accused of killing the most beloved black politician in the state. The papers ran story after story about her and her supposed obsession with Ban, which the police said was the reason for the shooting. I could not believe that anyone would believe such a story and I wondered why they were not doing a lot of digging into Savannah and David's background. Surely they had to know that the two of them came from the same town.

As a result of all the press, a reporter managed to sneak into Savannah's room posing as one of the hospital staff and managed to get pictures of her. Luckily she was caught by the guard and escorted out, but not before the camera was confiscated. Savannah wanted to sue the paper for the intrusion, but I told her to leave it alone; it was almost over and that she would be left alone to die in peace.

I wanted to ask her more about the events that led to Gina's suicide but she wasn't feeling well that day so I cut the visit short. Besides, I figured that I could get more out of Ronny Washington and he did seem eager, according to Bookie.

I got my chance the next day, the day before Savannah's scheduled bedside court appearance.

Bookie had arranged for me to go to Ronny Washington's home to talk with him. He did not want the press to get wind of the meeting so I waited until evening and Bookie and I rode together to his home.

Ronny Washington lives in Barrington, a northern suburb of Chicago, and it was late in the evening when we arrived. The guard at the gate was expecting us and as we drove up to the house, I could not help but be sad for him and for Gina. I realized that they would have had a beautiful life together. We were greeted at the door by Ronny and were surprised that he was cooking dinner for us. We made light conversation before our talk about Gina.

"Ronny, you have a beautiful home, my man," Bookie said as we entered. "Not bad for a young blood from Michigan City. You're doing great this season and I can see all sorts of endorsements in your future."

"Thanks, Mr. Lyman, I am blessed. And thank the two of you for making the trip up here. Did you have trouble finding the place?"

"First of all, it's Bookie, my friends call me Bookie. I'm old enough to be your older brother. And, no, the directions your manager gave us were fine."

"And you may call me Gemini, Ronny; I feel that a person who is so gracious to cook for me should call me by my first name."

"Gemini, I like to cook and entertain friends. I don't get to do it much so any excuse will do. Please join me in the kitchen."

We spent part of the evening watching Ronny cook and I set the table with Bookie over seeing everything, he is not that handy in the kitchen. The meal, which consisted of baked chicken with hunter's sauce, garlic mash potatoes, and green beans, was simply to die for. Ronny told us that the recipe for the chicken came from his mother who was planning to open a restaurant in Michigan City early next year. The wine he picked was the best that I had ever tasted and for dessert we had a peach cobbler that would make you smack the person next to you. We ended the meal with a toast to friends, past and future, and that is when the serious talk, the main reason for this meeting, began.

"Gemini, how is Savannah doing? I am sorry that I have not been up to see her, but my people are against it because of the publicity and they don't want bad press for me right now. Besides, they don't want the press brining up Gina's suicide. And to be honest with you, seeing Savannah right now, and knowing that she is ill, is too much for me. But, will you please tell her that I am thinking about her and my prayers are with her? Gina loved her, and I am only sorry that she did not live long enough to get to really spend time with Savannah as mother and daughter."

That last statement startled both Bookie and me.

"You know that Savannah is Gina's mother?" I asked.

"Yes, I know and I wanted to tell Gina but I never got the chance. Ban saw to that."

"What did he do, Ronny? How did he stop you from telling Gina?"

"By trying to make an issue about something from my past to Gina about me," there were tears in his eyes by now; he told Gina something about me that was not true. Thinking that it would break us up; and it did, but not the way he wanted it to. It killed Gina.

One year and two months before David Ban went to be with his ancestors.

David Ban sat in his office fuming and hurting at the same time. How could Gina do this to him? How could she leave him like this and marry that football player? What could he give Gina that she could not get from him? Love, money, respect, is that all she wanted? "I have been giving her all of this and more her entire life, and now she is going to leave me!" David said out loud, louder than he should have been. He was hurt too, hurt that the love of his life was leaving him for another man.

David was determined that he was going to stop it, but how? How could he stop something that everyone wanted but him? Even the Ghost had advised him to let the marriage take place, that it would be politically sound for him. It was time that he and Glenda have children of their own and let Gina live her life. That is what the Ghost wanted him to do. Well to hell with the Ghost and his dead momma, he was not going to let Gina end up with some damn athlete. Gina was his and that was the way it was going to remain. He had to get Ronny Washington out of the way, but how? How was he going to do it?

It did not take long for an idea to form in his sick mind. Yes, it could work, if he did things the right way. No one would know that he was behind this plan of his.

After forming the plan in his sick head, he set the plan in motion. First, he called a detective friend of his and asked him to come to his home for a meeting; it was personal, and he stressed the importance of secrecy. Mike Pampalone was a detective with a seedy reputation, and was also in the pocket of the Ghost. He would do anything for the right price and money was no object when it came to protecting Gina.

The plan was simple: find something on Washington that he could use to get Gina away from him. Ban was sure that there were some skeletons in Washington's closet and he was going to use them against him. And even if there weren't any skeletons, they could be created. That is really what Mike was good for, getting the "goods" on people.

The meeting took place that same evening at a restaurant outside of Hammond in a division called Hessville. Although Ban was well known throughout the state, he decided to pick this restaurant because of the location and the privacy the restaurant was known for. Besides, if someone recognized him, it would look like two old friends having a drink.

The meeting was brief, with Ban spelling out to Pampalone what he wanted done. He agreed to pay him five thousand dollars for information that was true and ten thousand for information that could be interpreted as true. He did not give the real reason for the assignment only that he felt that there was something about Washington that he did not trust and wanted him investigated before he married his sister.

Ban left the meeting that night feeling like a million dollars. His plan would work, his plans always did. Gina would not marry Ronny Washington. He knew the information that he would give to Gina would hurt her, but she would come to her big brother for comfort and he would be her one and only hero again. Wasn't love grand?

The next few days he had to endure the whirlwind of Gina and her wedding plans, he had to pretend to be interested when she showed him the place where the wedding and reception would be held. He even appeared to be in a good mood when that bitch of a mother of hers showed up and helped her with the dresses for the bridesmaids, the flowers, all the shit that women do to have a "dream wedding." He was just biding his time and when Pampalone called him, he would be ready to receive the news.

Washington was out of town at the moment; it was that season again. Ban hated sports, but Ronny he had just signed with a cereal company to endorse its new product and Ban had to admit that the punk ass was bringing in the dough. But it would not be enough, no amount was enough to let his Gina go.

Glenda was not really helping with the wedding, the stupid bitch was still trying to get him to have a baby, and he was still refusing her. He liked refusing her. He liked to see the look of anger on her face and knowing that there was nothing she could do about it, plus the fact that she liked being Mrs. David Ban; what woman wouldn't?

He got the call from Pampalone a week later. He would only tell David that he would be glad he investigated Washington; he did not have to make any of this up, it was all legit. They met at the same restaurant where the detective gave David an envelope containing the report he wanted.

He had struck gold! This was just what he needed to get that punk ass Washington out of his and Gina's life. He couldn't wait to bring her the news and watch the look of horror in her eyes. Yes, it would hurt him to see her in such pain, but after she turned to him for comfort, he would be okay. Then the only person he would have to deal with would be Savannah. At that was going to be as easy as she was at eleven years old.

He called Gina when he got to the house and asked to speak with her in private. The bitch Savannah and that wife of his were nowhere to be seen, so he had Gina all to himself. When she entered the study, he pretended to be upset by what he was going to tell her.

"Gina, honey, sit down, I have something I need to discuss with you."

"Look, David, I know that I am planning to spend a lot of money for my wedding so if it is the cost that you are worried about, I still have the trust money that Momma and Daddy left me."

"That's not what this is about, although it is about Ronny."

"What about Ronny, David; what do you want to discuss about Ronny?" David handed her the report and let her read it. She did not respond at first, but waited until she had read all of it before she spoke. And when she finally did speak, it was a side of Gina he had never seen and did not expect.

'WHERE DID YOU GET THIS, DAVID? WHAT ARE YOU TRYING TO DO?"

"Gina, I'm trying to save you from making a big mistake. This man is not to be trusted. I got it from a reliable sour-"

"I KNOW ALL ABOUT THIS, DAVID! RONNY TOLD ME BEFORE WE DECIDED TO COMMIT TO EACH OTHER. THIS IS A NONE OF YOUR BUSINESS, BIG BROTHER! WHERE DID YOU GET THIS, DAVID, I WANT TO KNOW NOW. AND WHAT IN THE HELL ARE YOU TRYING TO DO?" she said as she threw the report in David's face; the papers went all over the floor. David was so shocked and unprepared for Gina's reaction that his reaction was quick and primal; he slapped Gina and knocked her to the ground. But the brunt of his anger was yet to come.

"YOU STUPID BITCH, DON'T YOU GET IT? WASHINGTON IS A FAG, AN OUT AND OUT FAG. AND HE WAS RESPONSIBLE FOR A MAN KILLING HIMSELF. WHY DO YOU WANT TO BE WITH A FAG WHEN YOU CAN BE WITH A REAL MAN LIKE ME? I LOVE YOU, GINA, I ALWAYS HAVE AND NO MAN WILL EVER TREAT YOU THE WAY I WILL! YOU ARE MINE, HAVE ALWAYS BEEN MINE, AND WILL ALWAYS BE MINE!" The crazed look in his eyes told Gina that her brother was truly crazy and what he had just said made her sick to her stomach.

"YOU SICK SON OF A BITCH! I ALWAYS KNEW THERE WAS SOMETHING WRONG WITH YOU, EVEN WHEN I WAS A CHILD AND YOU WERE IN THE ROOM WITH THE TWINS. THE WAY YOU USED TO LOOK AT MY FRIENDS WHEN THEY

CAME OVER; I KNEW SOMETHING WAS WRONG WITH YOU! I AM SURPRISED THAT NO ONE HAS COME FORWARD AND LET THE WORLD KNOW JUST HOW BIG OF A HYPOCRITE YOU ARE, YOU SICK SON OF A BITCH! I AM LEAVING HERE TONIGHT AND NEVER COMING BACK!" Gina tried to make it to the door, but David caught her and threw her on the couch. Gina fought like a wildcat as David ripped off her clothes. There was no one to help her and she was no match for her brother's lustful rage. As he pulled her panties off and raped her all she could do was lay there in disbelief, her brother the man that was supposed to protect her, was raping her, taking her virginity; this was a nightmare!

David came to himself after it was over and realized that his daughter had been a virgin. How lucky he was to be her first, even if he had to force himself on her. He got up and zipped his pants and tried to comfort her as she got off the couch, trying to gather her clothes, "Oh, Gina," he thought, "we are one now. I have showed you how much I love you, now you can never belong to anyone else but me." He tried to reach for her, but the sudden pain in his groin made him bend over in pain, that pain was followed by the slap on his face and the force of Gina's slap sent him to the floor. By that time she had lost it and was kicking, scratching, and calling him names he did not even know she knew. Gina delivered blows all over his body before she grabbed her clothes and ran upstairs.

For a brief moment, he thought she was going to call the police, and that scared him. He did not know what to do if that happened, but for now, he had to get upstairs and get himself together before Glenda returned home and saw him. She would ask questions about his face and he did not feel like answering to that bitch. Besides, he needed to get himself together and apologize to Gina. Then they would patch things up and everything would go back to normal.

"So Ban tried to tell Gina that you were gay? How did you find out what he had done?" I was still in shock at how sick that son of a bitch Ban was.

"The detective that he hired to get that info on me contacted my people and tried to sell the information to me."

"What was the report about, Ronny? It's okay," I said, "this meeting stays between you, me, and Bookie. I give you my word."

"When I was in college, a guy that I knew was attracted to me and started harassing me to be with him. I told him that I was not into men and once or twice, I had to beat the shit out of him. He was some rich white kid who had a lot of problems and I guess he thought that his money would be enough to win me over. Jonathan Yager was his name and his parents were very wealthy people.

"Anyway, toward the end of school he got very aggressive with his advances so I finally went to the dean and complained. When he was called into the dean's office to account for his actions against me, he went crazy. He tried to kill himself that night; said it was all my fault. His parents were called and took him home, but that did not stop him. He called me so much in my room that I had to change phone numbers. It made me angry, because I had done nothing to encourage him. He was pretty sick."

"What happened to him?" Bookie asked.

"He killed himself a few months later, but not before he sent me all kinds of nude pictures of himself. He kept telling me that if I did not love him, life was not worth living; all kinds of sick shit like that. He sent me money, gifts, all kinds of things, but I always sent them back. I finally contacted his parents about what was going on and his father assured me that I did not have to worry; the harassing would stop. And it did. His father was rich enough to squash all of it so it never made the papers and did not interfere with me being signed with the Bears."

"If his father hushed everything up, how did the detective get a hold of the information?"

"Gemini, that is the million dollar question. I don't know, but he had it and tried to sell it to me. I guess in his own way, he was trying to tell me what Ban had on me and make some money off of me at the same time."

"How did Gina react?"

"She left me a message on my answering machine the night David told her. She said she told David to mind his own business and that she already knew. I made sure that I told her; I did not want any secrets between us. She also said to remember that she loved me. She said her brother was sick and that she was probably sick too, and that I would understand all of this one day. That was the last time I heard her voice. Ban would not let me come to the funeral, nor was I allowed to speak to him or Glenda. I do not know why Gina killed herself, and I hate that Savannah is charged with killing Ban; but I'm not sorry that he is dead."

"You would be surprised at the number of people who are as happy as you are," Bookie replied. "You would be surprised."

"We left Ronny's house around eleven for the hour and a half drive back to Indiana. I was quiet during most of the drive, but at one point, Bookie started a conversation that I knew would be coming sooner or later.

"All my Gemini, are you remembering to take your medication?"

"Yeah, sure I am. I'm right as rain."

"Then I can ask my next question. Why the hell are you pursuing this mess? Haven't you made your deal with the district assttorney? What the hell makes you go on with this? Leave this shit alone, Gemini, before it destroys you."

"I can't, Bookie, I just can't. I have to know what happened. I have this feeling in the pit of my stomach that there is more to this story than I have been told. I know that Savannah has kept shit from me; she wants to give me information a little bit at a time. She knows that I suspect Glenda Ban had a little more to do with this than they both let on. I just need to know the truth. Why did Gina kill herself? It couldn't have been because of what he had on Washington; Gina already knew the story so there was no reason for her to kill herself. Yep, there are pieces to this puzzle missing and I am determined to get to the bottom of this."

"Gemini, it's just like my grandmother, Mat, used to say, 'This shit will come out in the wash.' Just be cool, all y'all. It will come out."

"I am going to make sure that it does, Bookie, or my name ain't Gemini Alexis Jones."

"Don't forget Kremini and Remini, you got more than just yourself in there, all my Gemini. It's a lot of y'all inside that mind of yours."

"Then shut up and drive all of me home!" We both laughed and drove the rest of the way in silence.

The next day I received word that Savannah's hearing would take place the following day, and the press conference for the district attorney would take place today. After Savannah confessed to what she did, it would be all over. I decided that in the best interest of my client, I would remain silent about Ruthann. Besides, Omar Robinson was satisfied with the arrests and the police investigation. The consensus was that one of the officers involved had gotten sloppy and had destroyed evidence on a number of cases. The police and the district attorney's office would be so busy fighting every two-bit lawyer whose client felt that the evidence in their case was tampered with that they would be spending the next few months going over each and every case.

I had better things to do with my time anyway. I was riding on a hunch that Glenda Ban was somehow responsible for all of this, and I was determined to find out from Savannah. She owed me this. Being her defense lawyer had caused so many memories, memories that I had long ago been buried in the back of my mind, to surface, and I was living 1971 all over again.

I went to the hospital early and was surprised that Savannah was up and having a pretty good morning. That was good because I was going to press her today. I wanted to know the whole truth behind Gina's death, what role Glenda had played in all of this, and why was she taking the blame for all of it.

"Gemini, you're early. You still haven't grabbed that fine ass man Phillip "Bookie" Lyman and made him your man?" She was smiling and it made my heart glad to see that smile on her face. I wanted her to have as many good days as she was allowed to have, given the circumstances.

"We are and always will be friends, just friends. But I am not here to talk about my love life or lack of one, I am here to talk about you and a little word called the truth."

"Correction, you are here to be nosy and not let anything go. Let it go, Gemini. Please, for my sake and for the memory of Gina, let it go."

"I can't, Savannah; I can't. Too much has happened and I think it would do you some good to let all of this off your chest. I spoke with Ronny Washington last night, he told me about the information that Ban tried to use against him. I can imagine how that hurt Gina; to have the man she thought was her brother use it against her. But is that what happened to make her commit suicide?" I saw the look in Savannah's eyes and I knew there was something else, something that she had not told me but needed to get off her chest.

"It wasn't about the report that David had that killed her. It was what happened when she confronted him."

"What did that monster do?" I knew the answer before Savannah answered me.

"He raped her, Gemini." The tears were flowing now and the agony in her voice made me want to stop her from going on, but I couldn't. I just had to know the truth.

"She called me that night, the night that David confronted her about Ronny. And that, my cussing angel, was the last time I spoke to my baby."

Chapter 16

The night of Gina's suicide; one year and two months before David Ban went to his ancestors.

The phone woke Savannah up. Who in the hell was calling her this time of night? It was well past eleven o'clock and anyone who knew her knew that she went to bed early. When she saw Gina's name on the caller ID she was happy and alarmed at the same time. Something was wrong and her maternal instincts told her that Gina was in trouble and David Ban was the cause.

"Gina, what's wrong, honey? Is everything okay?"

"What makes you think that something is wrong? I just wanted to talk; that's all. Did I catch you at a bad time? Hell, it's eleven o'clock and you were probably sleeping, I'm sorry; I just wanted to talk."

Savannah was on full alarm now, there was something about the calmness is Gina's voice that disturbed her; but she decided to let Gina talk.

"Gina, it's okay, baby. Go ahead, tell me what's wrong?"

"How do you live in the same house with a person and not really know them? How have I lived in this house most of my life and not know just how twisted my brother really is? I guess I knew he had issues, but I did not know he was crazy. And now because of my ignorance, I have paid dearly for it."

"Gina, what's wrong? What did David do to you, did he hurt you?" Savannah was up now trying to get dressed and talk to Gina at the same time. "I'm coming over there right now. What did he do to you?"

"Oh, Savannah, my brother is crazy and I must be crazy too! You know that he always made me feel uncomfortable and uneasy. I never really could get close to him, even though we were brother and sister. I was too young to remember my parents, and he never wanted to talk about them. Just about us, me and him and the life that we were going to lead. I could never understand why he never mentioned Glenda in his plans, now I know. She wasn't part of his plan, just me, his sister; me." With that last statement, Gina started to cry a cry so hurtful, so full of aguish, that Savannah was determined that she was going over there and get Gina out of that house.

"Gina, I am on my way, stay on the phone with me, sweetheart. Please stay on the phone with me. I am coming and I am bringing the police with me."

"That won't be necessary, Savannah; I will be all right in a little while. You are so sweet to be concerned, but don't be. I will be fine. I just wanted to hear your voice and tell you that I love you, Savannah. I love you very much and thanks for the months of friendship. If you weren't so young, I would say thanks for being like a mother to me. You are, you know, like a mother to me; the mother I never had a chance to know. My own mother was distant from me, my father showed me all the love, but then God took them both and I had to live with David. Do you know how sick he is, Savannah? Do you know how many lives he has ruined? Mine, Ronny's, and Glenda's, especially Glenda's. Now I understand why she hates me so much, why she never wanted me around. Without knowing it, I was competition to her, just like if I was the other woman."

"Oh, my God!" Savannah thought. "Has he raped her? Oh, my God, I pray that he hasn't, I will kill him if he has."

"I am on my way, Gina. I don't care what you say! But please, baby, stay on the phone with me so I'll know you're okay."

"Savannah, I am so sorry that I bothered you. I will be okay. I promise I will."

"No you are not, David has hurt you and I am going to get to the bottom of it. Why don't you pack a bag and come home with me, you can stay as long as you want. And if you need more clothing, I will buy whatever you need. If you don't want to stay with me, I will take you to Ronny's house." By this time Savannah was in the car and racing down the street. Luckily for her, she did not live too far from the Bans.

"I can't go to Ronny's house, Savannah. Don't you understand, David has put a stop to that, to all of it. How can I face the man I love with the knowledge that I am spoiled goods?"

"Oh, my God, I was right, he raped her; the son of a bitch raped her!" Savannah thought. She was almost at the house. "Gina, I am calling the police and taking you to the hospital. I know, baby, I know what David has done, I know all too well. Please, baby, please stay on the phone until I get there!"

"I wish you had been my mother, Savannah; I wish that I had been raised by you. Not by David, who did nothing but lust after me. And not by Glenda, who hated me from day one. But you, I wished that I had been raised by you. Things would have been different. I could have married my Ronny, had the beautiful wedding that I always wanted. We would have had a wonderful life. I would have given you grandchildren; you should be surrounded by lots and lots of grandbabies running around the house."

Savannah was crying so hard now it was hard to drive, but she kept going. She was almost there. "Gina, you can still have that life. I would be proud to be your mother and the grandmother to your children. I would love to be surrounded by you and Ronny's children. We could be a real family. There is so much I want to tell you, honey, so much I want to share. Just give me time to get there and we can talk face to face. I will tell you a story, a story about a little girl who had to give up the one thing that meant more to her than anything or anybody. Please, Gina, please hold on, baby; please hold on. I'm coming, baby. Mama is coming."

It was as if Gina had not heard what Savannah just said. She kept talking and as Savannah drove up to the house, Gina hung up the phone.

The car barely had time to come to a stop before Savannah jumped out and raced to the Ban door. She pounded on the door until it was answered by the maid who informed her that the Bans were asleep. Savannah ran past her and was halfway up the stairs when she heard the shot. David and Glenda heard the shot too and jumped out of bed. They all raced down the hall to Gina's room.

Gina lay on the floor with a gunshot wound to her temple and blood oozing out onto the violet carpet. Savannah screamed and ran to her cradled her in her arms and rocked her dead child as David watched. He was in shock, and it took the maid's scream to bring him to his senses. Glenda had run back to their room to call the police.

Savannah looked up at David, saw the anguish in his face, and for one quick moment, almost felt sorry for him. Then the furry took over and she gently laid Gina down and stood to face her daughter's killer.

"You did this to her, you sick son of a bitch. You killed her, as God is my witness." She attacked David, who was still in shock and did not protect himself as she delivered the first blow to his groin. That was the second time he had been hit in the balls in one evening. The blow sent him to the floor, and that made it easier for Savannah to inflict the full force of her hatred on him. It took two guards to grab Savannah and hold her, but not before she put a hurting on David Ban. Glenda came back into the room and had the guards take Savannah out to the limousine. They were instructed to drive her somewhere, but were not allowed to tell her where; she was not there when the police arrived. David was bruised all over his body but told the police upon their arrival that he was fine.

The police were there for most of the night talking with David, Glenda and everyone else in the house. David told the police that his sister had been despondent over the past few days, but had not revealed to anyone the cause for her being depressed. He had been instructed to do so by the Ghost, who had even had David call his attorney to act as the family spokesperson.

The press had gotten wind of what had happened and had already staked claims on the Ban lawn. The attorney for the Bans arrived and began his job of protecting the family, only making basic statements pertaining to Gina's death and asking the press and the public to respect the privacy of the family. The autopsy would be performed to determine the cause of death and the press would be informed at the proper time

Savannah was taken to the home of Roy Karwatka by the guards, and put in the study. Shortly afterward, the Ghost, the man behind David Ban's political rise to power, entered the study; he was going to deal with her. What he did not know was that he had just met his match.

"You and that son of a bitch Ban had no right to bring me here. I want to go back to David's house and see Gina. I want to see her now."

"That won't be possible, Mrs. Wooten. The medical examiner has removed Gina's body and she is on her way to the morgue." That made Savannah cry, the pain was unbearable. Roy just stood there for a while and let her cry, he knew the pain she was feeling and why. He knew all about Savannah, it was his job to know. He motioned for the guards to leave, assuring them that things were okay, and then sat next to Savannah. His concern for her was genuine.

"Mrs. Wooten, I am sorry for the loss of your daughter. Yes, I know who you are, and I know that this is very painful for you. I too lost a child, so I know that pain that you are feeling. Plus, the fact that Gina never knew who you were is making all of this even more painful. But please, let me introduce myself. I am Roy Karwatka and again, Mrs. Wooten, I am sorry for your loss."

"Why are you keeping me here, Mr. Karwatka?"

"Please, call me Roy; my friends call me Roy."

"We are not friends, Mr. Karwatka. Any friend of David Ban's is no friend of mine. He killed my daughter and you want me to cover it up." The Ghost's reaction let her know she was right. "Yes, Mr. Karwatka, I know what you want, and I assure you that it is not going to happen. The whole world is going to know what he did to Gina and to me."

"And what about Gemini Jones? What about her and what happened to her? Are you willing to have that get to the press as well?"

"I have no intention of bringing Gemini or any of the other girls into this. This is not about them, it's about me and David Ban."

"But I will, Mrs. Wooten. I will leak it to the press; the whole, hurtful story. Then everyone will know about you, Gemini Jones, and what happened to her baby. Yes, Mrs. Wooten, I know what happened to Gemini's baby; that is my job to know. And if you promise not to go to the press, I will make sure that the secret of her baby will remain just that, a secret. However, if and when she ever wants to know about her child, I will give you that information to give to her. Don't think for one moment that I do not know what a monster David Ban is. But he is the most beloved black politician in this state; do you know what kind of power that gives me? I am not willing to give that power up for nothing or anyone. That includes you, your daughter, and that sick bastard. I will destroy you, Mrs. Wooten. And believe me, when I get through, David Ban will come out smelling like a rose. You, your friend Gemini, Ronny Washington, and Gina's memory will not fare as well. And what about your agency Highly Favored? I understand that your assistant director is running things in your absence and that the money from your husband's trust is helping to maintain it. But I will destroy that also, Mrs. Wooten. There is no end to my revenge if someone gets in my way. David Ban is on his way to becoming the first black governor of this state and I will not have anyone upset my plans for him. But I will tell you this, when I am finished with him, or if he somehow loses this election, which I am certain he will not, you may have him to do as you please. I will even provide you with the ammunition to do it with. Think about what I have said, Mrs. Wooten. You will get justice, when I say so."

His eyes told her that everything he had told her was the truth. Once he had her assurance that she would do nothing, she was taken back to her house. Her car, which she had driven to save Gina, was parked in front. She entered the house, went to the phone, and tried to call the Ban's home but got no answer. Her baby was dead and David Ban was the reason. "Well, Mr. Karwatka," she said out loud, "I will get my justice, WHEN I SAY SO!"

And that was the God's honest truth.

Chapter 17

I sat there in silence, too emotional to speak. Savannah had remained silent not only to protect Gina's memory, but to protect me and my child. Roy Karwatka knew where my child was and Savannah was protecting him also. She was giving her life for us, and I could not begin to repay this debt.

"So you see, Gemini, at first I was going to wait. I was going to let Roy Karwatka and David Ban make it all the way to the governor's mansion. But things don't always go as planned. I was not allowed to attend Gina's funeral, nor was Ronny, David made it a private family affair. I even went to the house a few weeks later just to get one item, a picture that Gina, Ronny, and I took on a trip to Green Bay one weekend to see Ronny play. But David would not let me have it. In fact, he tore it up right in front of me. I told him that I knew what he had done to Gina and he laughed and said that I had no proof. Besides, I had made a bargain with the devil, meaning Roy Karwatka, and there was nothing I could do to him. He was protected. I would have killed him then, but with my bare hands instead of a gun before the guards threw me out of the house. And somehow, when the press got wind of it, I heard the story was that I had made advances toward David and had come to the house to confront him after he rejected me. Roy Karwatka's people leaked that to the press. That was an out and out lie, and since his and Roy Kawatka's end of the bargain was not kept, I figured I would not keep mine either. So, with Glenda's help, I killed the son of a bitch. I wanted to do it in his house in the room where he raped my baby. But Glenda suggested that I do it out in the open where everyone could see it. That is why I chose the press conference."

"So, Glenda did help you with this, why are you taking all the blame?"

"You don't know the hell he put her through. Did you know that he passed her around to Nathaniel Hampton and Sherman O' Malley to further his political career? He even threatened the lives of her family if she did not sleep with these men. Then, after she did what she was told, he accused her of being a whore and refused to sleep with her. He even had a vasectomy before they married so that she would not get pregnant by him. So, when she ended up getting pregnant, he told her what he had done and made her get an abortion. The one thing she wanted most in the world was a child and he made her get rid of it."

"But she chose to stay in that marriage, no one forced her to stay. And why did she dislike Gina so much?"

"Because she knew how he felt about Gina, she knew he loved Gina more than he loved her; she just didn't know the depth and how twisted it was. He told her he was Gina's father after Gina died and that I was her mother. She felt as if he had killed her child and mine. That was our bond, the fact that we both lost children at his hands. And that is why I do not want any of this to come out, Gemini. Too many lives will be ruined and the memory of Gina will be tarnished even more. Let Glenda have her life, Gemini, she has suffered enough. I know she did not like Gina, but under the circumstances, you can understand why. If I can, surely you can. But as far as I am concerned, she redeemed herself when she let me come to the press conference with her as her guest and ordered the guards not to search me. After all, I was there in memory of Gina. At least I had a chance to see and hold my child; Glenda did not. And you know how that is, Gemini; not being able to hold your child, to be with your baby. Let it rest, Gemini. Let it all die with me."

I could tell that this talk had tired her out, so I left shortly afterward and promised that I would think about what she had told me.

I got to the office around ten and was told that someone named Ms. Summer had called and left a message for me to get back with her. I knew immediately who it was. It was Ruthann Loggins, but I was not surprised she had called, on the contrary, actually. I had been expecting it.

Even though I was expecting her call, I was still not prepared to return it. There was so much at stake; Savannah wanted to die in peace and save Gina from further scrutiny by the press. I owed that to my client. But there was still a part of me that wanted to talk with Ruthann and somehow thank her for what she attempted to do for Savannah. Besides, I wanted to see my friend again; it brought me that much closer to my past, and to the prospect that my son was somewhere alive and well. At least I hoped he was.

I decided that I would call her after the press conference and the hearing. That way Savannah would already be sentenced. The press conference went as planned. The district attorney, Omar Robinson, informed the public about Savannah's bargain and that his office was satisfied that justice had been done.

I prepared for the sentencing hearing on the following day and thought about how my conversation would go with Ruthann. Should I take Bookie with me? After all, part of his duty was to protect the attorneys if need be and serve as a witness, but I decided not to involve him. This talk would be between Ruthie and me, two women who once shared a horrible situation and had each been scarred by what happened, and affected by it in different ways.

The day of Savannah's court date was upon us. We were scheduled to meet at the hospital; the judge, Omar Robinson, myself, and a court stenographer. For the record, Omar informed the judge that a deal had been reached and then Savannah went on record to say that she, in fact, had been responsible for the death of David Ban and how it was done. She apologized to the court and to the family of David Ban, which seemed to please both the judge and Robinson. Savannah looked almost relieved to have everything over; I know I was. And as agreed, the judge sentenced Savannah to remain in the hospital until she either got better and could be moved to jail where she would receive care there, or until her death.

The press was waiting outside when Omar and I left the hospital and we each made our statements. Omar was satisfied that justice had been served, vowed to continue to fight for the people of this city, blah, blah, blah. In my statement to the press, I stated that my client was gravely ill and wanted to spend the remainder of her time in peace; then I returned to the office.

Quinn was still in the office when I returned and wanted to see me. He poured us both a glass of the apple juice that he makes himself on his farm in Michigan, a place he likes to retreat to whenever possible.

He told me that the partners were satisfied with the outcome and told me that he did not want to see me in the office for the rest of the week. I did not leave right away. I managed to finish some paper work, and as soon as it was done, so was I. I decided that I was going to treat myself that afternoon by having a manicure and pedicure and buying a cute little blue jean outfit that I had my eye on.

I got home a little after nine that evening. Kyrra was waiting for me and, as usual, wanted to be the center of attention. I turned on the TV just in time to catch the evening news. After undressing and changing into my doo-doo brown t-shirt with the holes in the front, I sat down with a bottle of wine, no glass. I was going to be real ghetto tonight and drink right out of the damn bottle. I wanted to get drunk and forget. Damn my medication; damn that I was bipolar and did not need to be drinking period; damn that I had court tomorrow. I wanted to get drunk, and pass out. Now I said it, just pass out. But what I saw on the news changed my mind real fast. I dropped the whole bottle of wine on the floor, but that didn't matter.

What mattered was the woman on the news whose name was Mattie Holman. She was making a statement that she had been the mistress of the late David Ban and that the affair had started when she was fifteen.

I reached for the phone to call Bookie but then the phone rang and I picked it up. It was Bookie; he must have been watching the same newscast.

"I told you the shit was going to come out of the wash, didn't I, baby girl? Are you watching channel seven?"

"Hell yeah, I am; and this is just the beginning, I am sure. Young girls are going to come out of the woodwork about Ban. This is going to upset Savannah, now the focus will be on Gina again."

"Yeah, the press is probably going to speculate that Gina killed herself because of David somehow being a child molester."

"And dammit, Bookie, they would be right on the money! Damn, I knew that there was going to be some backlash behind his death but I did not think it was going to be this bad. I had better be at the hospital in the morning when Savannah wakes up; I don't want her to have to hear this alone."

"I don't think this is something that was done to hurt Savannah, Gemini. I mean, look at the woman. She obviously thinks that she can make some money by telling her story. And you are right; other women will probably come out and claim he had sex with them too. But I think this will die down. Maybe not now, but in a few weeks, it will all blow over. But it's over for you, baby girl. It is over for you."

"Phillip Bookie Lyman, you're right. But I am still going to be at the hospital early tomorrow just to be on the safe side. Now my ass is tired and I wants to go to bed."

"You sure can sound ghetto when you want to, all my Gemini. That is not the way to please a man." He was teasing me.

"I know that. And when I find one, I'll know how to talk," I shot back.

"Why you hurt me like that, baby girl. You are no earthly good, Gemini Jones. No earthly good at all."

"And I love you too, Bookie Lyman." Then all he heard was a dial tone.

The phone woke me up at 2:00 a.m. It was Mrs. Gill to tell me that Savannah had passed away in her sleep and that she was at peace. I sat up in my bed long after I got off the phone with her, partly out of being sleepy and partly out of disbelief. Savannah's mother informed me that she had died shortly after 1:00 a.m., and that if I wanted to come to the hospital to see her, I had better come now. She had made all of her funeral arrangements and the funeral home would be there shortly to take the body.

I dressed quickly and called Bookie to ask if he could drive me to the hospital; I told him about Savannah. He arrived about fifteen minutes later and drove me to the hospital to see my friend.

We were met by Savannah's parents and were given permission to go in and say good-bye. She had suffered a heart attack and had died very quickly. As I entered the room, I could feel the coldness of death and the feeling was too much for me. The tears began flowing down my face to confirm my feelings.

Savannah lay on the bed and it looked as if she had a smile on her face. Her mother had combed her hair and the nurses had laid her arms to each side so that she looked more like she was asleep, and in a way, she was. She was asleep while her spirit was with Gina. I sat by the bed and took her hand, which was cold, and cried like a child, cried like I never did before. But it was a cry that I needed to wash away all the bad memories. Memories of being at Mamie Wells's home, of having to give up my child, and finally, of my friend, the bravest person I knew. She was one of the few people with enough heart to die having people believe bad things about her to keep them from knowing what bad things had happened to her and to Gina.

"Miss Jones, I want a word with you." I turned to see Elder Gill standing at my side. They say in the press that my daughter was stalking Ban and was upset by his rejection of her. Why would they say such a thing? And now they got that woman on TV saying that she was his mistress since she was fifteen. What kind of monster was David Ban?"

"He was a demon, Elder Gill," I said. "He was a demon and he preyed on those who did not know any better. Now he is in the deepest, hottest part of hell. Savannah is with Gina now and both are at peace. Now it is up to us to find peace also, Elder Gill. That is what Savannah would want for all of us, to find peace and move on."

I sat with Savannah's parents until it was time to move the body to the funeral home. It was hard watching her being placed in the hearse, but I knew that she would want me there. After all, I was her angel and I had always been there with her, through thick and thin. Now I would be with her in death.

I informed the district attorney's office about Savannah, and Omar was genuinely concern about her parents and me. I told him that her parents and I would be fine. I had Bookie take me home and later I went to the funeral home with her parents to help with the arrangements.

The funeral took place a few days later. All of the employees of Highly Favored and a lot of the clients were in attendance. I noticed that Ruthann Loggins was also in attendance; and although we did not speak to each other, the looks that we exchanged told it all. We were both grateful to have known Savannah and we would both have to move on with our lives. She had to face a trial, and I had to face trying to locate my son. I had decided to do it and make things right. I wanted to do this for myself, my son, and for Savannah.

Savannah was dead and my heart was broken.

Part of me understood how she felt, wanting to be with her daughter. But part of me had wanted her to fight, just as she had done all her life. Savannah had overcome so much in her lifetime and had done so well; she had even been given the chance to get to know her daughter.

Two weeks later, as I was preparing to leave the office for the day, I received a package from the executor of Savannah's estate.

The manila envelope contained an even smaller envelope which contained a letter. I hesitated before reading the letter; I wasn't sure what was inside, and the thought that Savannah had written me before she died made me even sadder than I was before I got the package.

As I read the letter, I understood just how much my friendship had meant to her, but the pain that I felt was unbearable. She had found out what I had been unable to do; not out of not having the resources, but out of fear. She knew where my child was and it sickened me.

Gemini,

I know that you are angry with me for not fighting to stay alive. Please under-stand I am tired, tired of being without my Gina, my baby. The pain that I have suffered since she died makes it impossible for me to go on. If you get this letter, it means that I have gone on and I am with my baby girl now.

When I first arrived at Mamie Wells's house, I was scared and alone. I had no one, not even God, or so I thought. But little did I know that God was with me; he sent me a crazy, fifteen-year-old with a mouth like a sailor and the heart of a saint. A fierce female warrior who would make even Queen Izinga of Africa proud; he sent me you. You made those days with Bitch Wells bearable, and for that, I will always love you and consider you the sister that I never had. You may not know just how strong you are, but I am here to tell you that if it had not been for you, I would have killed myself while I was in that hell.

So, the only way that I can repay you for what you did for me is to give you the greatest gift I can: your child. Yes, Gemini, I know where your child is. But it may hurt you to know what happened to him.

Your son's name is Vincent Wells. Yes, Gemini his last name is Wells. Mamie kept him for herself and raised him as her own child. I guess it was her way of getting back at you for the times that you two fought and for helping me and the others who were victims of her cruelty.

From the information that I received, he is doing fine; but to be raised by Bitch Wells, I know that he has some problems.

Go to him, Gemini; let him know who you are. I know that there is a hole in your heart, a hole that has never been filled. I know because I had the same hole until I saw Gina and had a chance to spend time with her. I should have told her in the very beginning who I was, but I was afraid, and that cost me the only other person who ever meant as much to me as you.

That hole will never go away until you have faced him and Mamie and tell him your story.

You must also confront Mamie. She is still alive, but lives in Chicago now. That is where Vincent is also. I have enclosed the addresses for both of them; use it when you are ready to do so. This is my gift to you, my cussing angel, my sister, my friend. I hope that I am doing the right thing by telling you all of this.

I am certain that you will be hearing from Roy Karwatka again; when, I am not sure, but you can bet on it that you will. Be careful of him, he is a very power-ful man and I know that he was upset about how things turned out. I ruined his plans for David and I am afraid that you might pay the price.

I pray that you can be united with your son and live the rest of your life in happiness. And for your sake, grab that fine detective that works in your firm and make him yours. Even Stevie Wonder can see that he cares a great deal for you, *despite your challenges and age. You deserve love in your life; and if it comes in a younger package, so be it. Life is short and happiness is shorter. Go for it, girl-friend. Remember, you are "Highly Favored!"*

God bless you. I love you, my sista.

Savannah

The tears were flowing as I finished the letter. I was feeling a variety of emotions, but the one that stood out was anger; anger at Bitch Wells for keeping my baby. God only knows what she did to him. God only knows what she told him about me, if she told him about me at all.

I decided that at this point, I would do nothing. I would wait until I could clear my mind and figure out what to do. But I did know this: I had to even the score. I was going to get Mamie Wells. And God help anyone who tried to stop me.